Sodor Reading Between the Lines

Christopher Awdry

AF727621

Full-Steam-Ahead

Full-Steam-Ahead

A word from the publisher

Why is Thomas Blue?
What did the Rev'd Awdry think of the TV Series?
Which Story does Percy first appear in?

These are just three of the many questions, which are asked regularly, and the answer to these and many others are here. *Reading Between the Lines* builds on the popular book published by the Rev'd W Awdry and his brother George in 1987 and now out of print. While covering some of the history of the Island of Sodor, home of Thomas the Tank Engine and his many friends, and listing the friends created by the Awdrys, father and son, this new book concentrates mainly on answering those questions and setting out, story by story, the location, origin and story out-line for every tale so far published in what has become a "Classic" series of children's books.

Yet despite their classic status many of these books have been out of print for up to 10 years, a scandalous situation in many people's eyes. Efforts to improve this are meeting with some success but there is more work to be done – *Reading Between the Lines* pulls no punches in setting out where the author believes the problems lie.

Christopher Awdry, with his father's encouragement, took over the writing of the best-selling Railway Series in 1983. By 1996 he had completed 14 titles, in addition to many Thomas spin off books as result of the TV series, before the publisher, as you will read here, decided to change direction. The author is greatly saddened that he can currently point to only three of about 42 books, which might be available for an author's signature. In 2005 he continued to tour at home and abroad, however, visiting Days Out with Thomas and other events, hoping to help to restore the classic Thomas stories to a new generation of fans.

However in 2014, a life of worldwide book tours and railway events began to take its toll, that coupled with unwanted media intrusion that left Christopher wanting to take a step back from the limelight and shy away from public events. There are after all, only so many answers you can give to some of the more, shall we say, 'daft', questions that were being asked by certain media outlets. Suffice to say, people's attitudes in the 1950's and beyond are far different to the views held today. Not that that is a bad thing, change can be good, but can you really take a Children's book series and make it political? Some thought they could, and that's when Christopher decided that, for the best of his family and health he would finally enjoy a life of retirement in Dorset.

However, life has a funny habit of turning things on its head, and one day, whilst clearing out an old garage full of old boxes he came upon a collection of his father's things. And inside he found a treasure trove of documents and memorabilia that pertained to his father's books. Armed with this new horde of information, and deeply saddened at how much people were paying for his original 2005 book online, he decided to re-publish the book, which brings us to the work you now hold in your hand...

2025 is the 80th anniversary of the publication of the first book in the Railway Series and it seems a fitting occasion as any to update his 2005 publication, thus forming this 20th anniversary edition and adding details of his further two additions to the Series.

We, and Christopher, hope that you enjoy...

Other Works

Also by Christopher Awdry, though not part of the Railway Series are:-

The Eastbourne Miniature Series.
LOTI and the Enchanted Forest.
LOTI and the Lost Locket.
Railway for Sale.
Luke Goes Flying.
Heave Ho Hamish.
The Chips Express.

Copyright © [2025] by [Full-Steam-Ahead]

All rights reserved.

ISBN – 978-1-9193093-0-9

No portion of this book may be re-produced in any form without written permission from the publisher.

For more information please go to www.Full-Steam-Ahead.co.uk

First published in 2005 by Sodor Enterprises.

Second edition edited and published by Full-Steam-Ahead 2025.

Publishers note – Please be aware that this book contains thoughts, phrases or terminology used in the past (1940 – 1980) that then were acceptable, however by todays standards, could could offence. Reader discretion is advised.

Front cover and map on back page – The map of Sodor drawn in Ordnance Survey Format courtesy of Peter Edwards (Railway Series Illustrator 1963 -1972)

Dedication

For Thomas lovers, everywhere

Contents

Introduction

My Father told the story of how Thomas the Tank Engine came about more times than he could count, and I have now run out of fingers too, but I have no doubt that even this particular telling will be a long way from the last. At the age of two and a quarter, durinq the autumn of 1942, I became ill with measles. Measles was regarded then with perhaps more seriousness that it appears to warrant today, and my fate was three weeks of quarantine, in a darkened room. My father, given the task of amusing me in this extremity, and having exhausted the traditional nursery rhymes of the period, used a rhyme he recalled from his own childhood:-

Early in the morninq
Down by the station,
See the little engines
All in a row.
Along comes the driver,
pulls the little lever.
Peep, peep, chuff, chuff,
Off we go.

He illustrated this rhyme with his own rather rudimentary drawings, then made up answers to the questions I asked about them. He then realised that he could develop the answers he concocted into a story, and we were off. By the time I recovered there was a first story about Edward, another about Henry which developed from another rhyme in a similar way, and a third which began "One of the engines in Edward's shed was called Gordon." This was based on a tale that he had heard (so he said) from one of the local railwaymen – King's Norton Station was about half a mile down the road – of engines stalling with goods trains on the nearby Lickey Incline, a notoriously steep gradient.

For Christmas that year he made me a toy tank engine out of some odds and ends he had to hand and painted it blue, adding also a number 1 on the side tank, not because it was the first engine he had – it wasn't – but for the authentic and practical reasons that engines had numbers and 1 was the easiest to paint. On request he then made up stories about this engine too, in the process naming it Thomas the Tank Engine.

Any story told *al fresco* rarely comes off the tongue identically at each telling, and I soon began to notice this, stopping Father when I thought he was going wrong. His reaction was to write the stories down so that he could read them and we would therefore get, as he used to say: "...the same version every time." Soon after, my mother, finding, as she thought, no books in the shops suitable for me, urged him to 'do something' with his stories, and eventually, in May 1945, *The Three Railway Engines* was published, to be followed by the four stories about Thomas as *Thomas the Tank Engine* the next year. The story of how this came about can be found in much greater detail than there is room for here, in *The Thomas the Tank Engine Man*, by Brian Sibley, published by Heinemann in 1995 and given a second edition by Lion Hudson in 2015. But this sadly may now be out of print, although I am reliably informed it is still available as an ebook.

From that time, at a rate of more or less one a year, other titles followed until 1972, by which time my father had written 26 books and 105 stories – there are four stories in each book but five in *Henry the Green Engine*. My own efforts began, with Father's encouragement, in 1983 and continued until 2011, by which time the total number in the series had reached 42. Despite the publisher's reps telling me during the 1990's that "...they didn't have to sell them..." all but 14 had been allowed to go out of print by 1998 and have remained so except for a boxed edition of father's 26 titles produced in 2002 and the special collection in a single volume, again Father's 26 books, which sells well but is currently (October 2025) also out of print. As regards sales of the Railway Series, I can only say that my Wife and I have had no difficulty whatsoever in selling the 14 titles which are currently available at any charity function we are invited to.

A book which told the story of the development of the Island of Sodor – on which the engines run – was written by my father and his brother George and published in 1987. It was called *The Island of Sodor, its People, History and Railways:* this too has been out of print for some time, and even copies through dealers are becoming scarce and expensive. My father lamented the fact that so much had to be left out of this book in order to be able to publish it an an acceptable price: it was with the aim, in part, of filling that gap, and also to mark (at the time of first publication 2005) the 60th anniversary of the publication of that first title in the Railway Series, that Sodor Enterprises published this volume. Our original book was slimmer than my father's original, but contained updates to some of the answers to the many questions that came to us hourly by the internet, letter or in the field. (Although the later not so much nowadays!)

All the engines appearing in the titles of the Railway Series – note it has never officially been the 'Thomas' series – are described here, and any page numbers quoted apply to the original edition of the books concerned. The antecedents of characters developed by televison/film interests in the years after 1984 are not known to this writer and are perhaps better left to some later historian. Some of the most frequent questions are: "Which story does so and so first appear in?" and "Where can I find the story of (say) Percy and the Scarf?" A large part of this work is aimed specifically to satisfy the where, what and how of these questions: It should be read not as a substitute but complimentary to the earlier volumes and we sincerely hope will prove a worthy successor and addition to it.

The Island and its Railways

The development of the Island

The Island of Sodor was not entirely a figment of my father's imagination. During the early 1950s he had been getting a great deal of correspondence from various people – not just children – who wanted to know where, for instance, Henry's tunnel was, or the location of Thomas's branch line. He began to feel that he needed somewhere concrete, as it were, at which to fix them, but searches by both he and his brother found nowhere (other than some totally unsuitable and virtually uninhabited wastes in the north of Scotland) which did not already possess railways. This of course, was before the Beeching Report appeared and was implemented – they would have a much easier task now!

As Secretary of the Ely Diocesan Sunday School Council he was invited, in 1951, to preach at a Sunday School festival service at Douglas, on the Isle of Man. While there he became aware of the proper name of the See – the Bishopric of Sodor and Man, and during the flight back to Manchester airport, or so he told us, it occurred to him that if he were to drop an island into the sea between the English mainland and the Isle of Man he could, at a stroke, not only use it as a basis for his railway system, but give the Bishop of Sodor and Man the other half of his Diocese back. Let me at this stage hasten to point out that there is , in fact, a genuine historical reason for the name, and this is dealt with in the Frequently Asked Questions section – see below.

So the Island of Sodor was born, and cartographers among our readers will find that it comprises, in fact, a westward extension of Walney Island, off the Cumbrian coast at Barrow, even including the community of Vickerstown thereon – though we in Sodor spell it Vicarstown. The map on the cover of this book – and shown in the last pages of this book – was painted to set Sodor in its Ordnance Survey context, and we are greatly indebted to its artist, the late Peter Edwards, for his willing permission to use it.

My father and his brother now began to put various bits of the jigsaw together. George, who was at the time the Librarian at the National Liberal Club in London, had ideal opportunities for historical and other research and it was he who supplied much of the detail, while Father himself took on the 'literary' side of the task. Many items of various sorts came together: history, much of it based on Manx or Norse records, geography and of course, the railway themselves. All were carefully annotated and nothing was proposed that did not have the appropriate causality – the same meticulous methodology, in fact, that was being put into the stories themselves. The snag about this type of approach, of course, is that parameters become limited, and this has led to some bizarre TV stories which do not wish to be restricted in this way – a canal for example, where there has never been a need for one and elaborate dockside cranage at a port which would have nothing like the amount of business to warrant it. It can, and has, been argued that a child does not appreciate such niceties, but for one who had made such a point of authenticity and truth in his tales, such flights of fancy left a bitter taste.

The Railways of the Island

The Railways of the Island of Sodor were, as my father envisaged them, accurate in both history and railway regulations, and logical in their situation. The earliest standard gauge railway on the Island was the Sodor & Mainland Railway, built to link the Island with mainland Britain – it was not a successful venture and by 1901 all but one (Neil) of its locomotives (there had been only three of them anyway) had been scrapped, though the Company itself remained dormant. The Tidmouth, Knapford & Elsbridge Railway was begun in 1883 and became renamed as a Light Railway in 1908, when an extension to Tidmouth was finally made and steam superseded horse power as the motive force. A W Dry was the contractor who built the line, and his young assistant was a Mr Topham Hatt.

The Wellsworth & Suddery Railway. a coastal line between Suddery and Brendam, was opened in 1870, but in 1908 the harbour at Suddery failed and the Company threw in its lot with the TK&ELR to reach the port of Tidmouth. A joint committee worked the lines from 1912, but in 1914 all three standard gauge lines were amalgamated as the North Western Railway when concerns were felt against possible danger from Ireland, the line being seen as a strategic coastal defence.

The branch line from Killdane to Peel Godred was built by the NWR as a light railway in 1923, and some of its gradients are therefore heavy. It was agreed that it would be worked by electric traction, and a passenger service is maintained using multiple units. Freight to and from the Aluminium Works at Peel Godred is heavy and locomotives similar to Class 86 and 87 are used. There has been talk of electrifying the remainder of the route across the Island to Barrow but since a change of locomotive would be necessary there anyway – or at least until the route from Carnforth to Barrow is also electrified ("Fat chance!" do I hear you say?) – The Fat Controller has shelved the plan.

The oldest railway on the Island is the Skarloey Railway which began as a 2ft 3in gauge horse tramway in 1806 run by the Crovan's Gate Mining Company. It ran to mines on Ward Fell which yielded copper. In 1865/6 the line was converted for steam traction, and two locomotives, *Skarloey* and *Rheneas* (the correct and official pronunciation of this name uses a short first syllable, on which the principle emphasis should be placed) were delivered. The line was successful for a while but after the mines closed in the 1940s and up to 1966, things were difficult. Now, however, run primarily as a tourist line, the Skarloey Railway is busier than it has ever been and keeps its eight locomotives well employed.

The Culdee Fell Railway, a 2ft 7.5in rack railway up the mountain after which it is named, opened in 1900 and is eight miles long. It runs for tourists during the summer months. The Mid Sodor Railway is actually older, having been opened in 1880 between the sea at Arlesburgh (pronounced Arlsburg) and mines at Peel Godred. The previous volume is a little coy about what sort of mines these actually were; slate was in fact the predominant commodity but there was some business in general good also. In 1946 the last of the slate mines became worked out and the line closed. Like the Skarloey, the Mid Sodor Railway was also gauged at 2ft 3in. Twenty years later the trackbed for ten miles inland from Arlesburgh was relaid with a railway of 15-inch gauge, partly to cater for a growing tourist industry and partly to serve granite quarries at Marthwaite. The stone from the quarry has particular notable 'weedfree' qualities, and the Fat Controller uses it as railway ballast. This 15-inch gauge line is now known as the Arlesdale Railway.

Locomotives and other characters

Standard gauge

The only locomotive from the early companies to be illustrated in a book is *Neil*, a survivor from the Sodor & Mainland Railway. He makes a very brief appearance in *Very Old Engines*, (p.11) and is a typical contractors' engine of the period – the story takes place in 1865 – but it is hard to say which factory he might have come from. The SMR was a Company whose attitude to records could be described as casual, and details of Neil's acquisition have, sadly, been lost. Contrary to rumours of Neil's demise, he is in fact still in working order and believed to be now part of the recently (2025) formed Crovan's Gate Preservation Society.

A number of engines survive from the North Western period and later. In number order they are:-

Thomas (1)

As with Neil, the record as to how he reached the Island is uncertain. He is one of the Billinton – designed 0-6-0 tank engines, Class E2, of the London, Brighton & South Coast Railway, one of a half dozen or so which were fitted with an extension at the front end of the watertanks for dockside working at Southampton. Southampton or not, Thomas seems to have arrived rather mysteriously in 1915 – perhaps it was a wartime mix-up – and, so the story goes, by 1920 both his driver and fireman had married local girls and didn't much want to go back to the south coast of England. The Fat Controller bought Thomas for a nominal sum, and after a spell as shed-pilot at Vicarstown, he came to Wellsworth, where, in his rescue of James (see *Thomas the Tank Engine*, below) he proved himself to be a Really Useful Engine. His reward was to be put in charge of the Ffarquhar branch, which runs to that village from a junction at Knapford. Various Thomas look-alikes can be found on our 'heritage' railways, but none is identical – the last of the original engines was cut up in the 1950's.

Edward (2)

Edward's journey to Sodor was shorter that Thomas's but they seem to have arrived at about the same time. He is a 4-4-0 of the 'Large Seagull' class introduced on the Furness Railway, which ran the Cumbrian Coast line in 1896. Some say he came over the bridge from Barrow on official business but couldn't somehow find his way back again, but the official story is that he was borrowed during a locomotive crisis and later bought, like Thomas, for a 'nominal sum'. He has been extensively modified while on the Island, and the theory that in the old days he had difficulty making steam is certainly not true now. He is in charge of the Brendam branch, which runs from a junction at Wellsworth, often described in the stories as 'Edward's station'. None of Edward's original Class have survived.

Henry (3)

There have actually been, in effect, two Henrys – for the story of why this is please see the Frequently Asked Questions section, under 'Engines', Suffice here to say that since Henry's return from Crewe he has been, to use my father's expression, "a reformed character". He now looks very much like a Stanier Class 5, of which several examples can be seen at preserved lines up and down the country. It is the current Fat Controller's hope that the Works at Crovan's Gate may yet be able to tap into what could be a lucrative market for the supply of spares for these heritage line locomotives.

Gordon (4)

Gordon is sometimes compared with that most famous of all Gresley 'Pacifics', No.4472 *Flying Scotsman*. In fact a true likeness is now pretty loose, but according to notes my father made when talking to Sodor railwaymen, Gordon stems from a prototype experimental engine built in 1922 when Gresley was projecting his new Class A1 (as they were then) 4-6-2s for the Great Northern Railway. The prototype was never used in traffic by that Company, and was set aside when the production run began. Then, in 1923, it was sold to the North Western Railway along with a spare boiler. Which is where his similarity to Flying Scotsman ceases, because in 1939, during the course of a heavy overhaul at Crewe, his conjugated valve gear, as originally fitted by Gresley, was removed and a two-cylinder chassis of the Fat Controller's own devising substituted.

James (5)

In 1912/13 George Hughes of the Lancashire & Yorkshire Railway built a class of 0-6-0 tender engines for general mixed-traffic use. It was found that when running at speed, as they had of course to do on passenger duties, they became nose-heavy. Hughes experimented by providing one of the engines with a pony-truck, but the experiment was not a success. In 1923 the LMS sold the engine to the North Western Railway. Crovan's Gate has solved many of the engine's inherited problems, including replacing the wooden brake-blocks with which James had been fitted – ref: *Thomas the Tank Engine*, p60. No locomotives of James's original type survive.

Percy (6)

The Fat Controller needed a shunting engine (ref: *Troublesome Engines* p40) and bought an appealing hybrid from a factory on the Mainland. Percy defies certain identification, and it sometimes appears that he was put together by using any appropriate parts that came to hand – components from both Avonside of Bristol and Hunslet of Leeds are among the commonest but by no means exclusively. It is probably the former of these two major concerns that can claim most responsibility. After purchase Percy saw service first in the yard at Tidmouth, then assisting with the construction of the harbour near Knapford Junction. He is now in charge of freight traffic on the Ffarquhar branch. Several Percy look-alikes can be found on preserved railways but none is identical.

Toby (7)

Toby is a 0-6-0 'tram' engine of Great Eastern Railway origin. the Fat Controller met him, as a boy, while on holiday in East Anglia in 1951 (ref: *Toby the Tram Engine* p8) and his grandfather was later able to purchase him for use on the Ffarquhar quarry branch when Toby's East Anglia line was closed (ref: *Toby the Tram Engine* p34). My father has explained that he was probably No.68221 originally, one of a batch of three J70 class locomotives built in 1914. His small watertank has been a source of embarrassment on more than one occasion, but used in the normal way he has proved himself invaluable. He brought with him from East Anglia Henrietta, a wheeled coach (see below). There are no genuine survivors of this locomotive class.

Duck (8)

Duck makes his first appearance in Percy the Small Engine (ref: p20), when he is acquired to to take charge of Tidmouth yard. Although his official number is 8 this is not used on the railway: Sir Topham Hatt 1 had served an engineering apprenticeship at Swindon, and when Duck arrived in 1955 Sir Topham Hatt II appreciated his father's Great Western sympathies by permitting Duck to retain his cast GWR-type numberplates. The number shown is 5741, though the GWR has stipulated that this might not, in fact, be the number with which he was allocated when built in 1929 to a design by C B Collett. Duck – whose real name, incidentally, is Montague – has proved himself a valued member of the loco-stud, and in recognition of this, when the Fat Controller re-opened the Arlesburgh branch in 1967, he put Duck in charge. It is a responsibility which Duck takes very seriously. Several of Duck's relations can be found on preservation sites around the country.

Donald (9)/ Douglas (10)

Identical ex-Caledonian Railway 0-6-0 tender-engines of MacIntosh's '812' Class arrived on the Island of Sodor in 1960. Sir Topham had, in fact, ordered only one, No.57646, but, anxious not to be separated from his brother, No.57647 came along too: it is thought – unofficially, of course – that their crews, (who were related) deliberately confused the paperwork so that no-one could tell which was which – ref: *The Twin Engines* p8 and following. The upshot was that Sir Topham accepted both, named them Donald and Douglas respectively, and to show that they belonged, gave them a blue livery instead of the BR black in which they had arrived. They have taken charge of freight working on the Island and transformed it, and the Fat Controller considers them one of his better bargains. One example remains of this class and although based at the Strathspey Railway, is on long term loan to the Spa Valley Railway in Kent.

Oliver (11)

Like Duck, Oliver is allowed to wear his Great Western number, 1436, though, again like Duck, there is some doubt as to whether this is original. Also like Duck, he is to a design by C B Collett, a 0-4-2 tank engine intended for branch line passenger duties, but three years younger having been introduced in 1932. In 1967 his crew, alarmed that Oliver's branch line in the West Country was about to be closed, plotted to escape to the Island of Sodor, along with an auto-coach called Isabel and a Great Western brake van called Toad. Douglas comes across them in Barrow yard and the two crews colluded to smuggle the fugitives across to the Island. After an extensive overhaul, Oliver was put to work on Duck's branch line and the two Great Western locomotives now work happily together.

Phillipa/Emma

It was The Fat Controller's intention, now that the Other Railway has been overtaken by Privatisation, to purchase them with a view to giving Suddrians a faster London service. His plan is now in place, and the pair now do a complete round trip every day, something barely attainable hitherto. They are the twin power cars of a High Speed Train (HST for short) and first appeared as casualties in *Gordon the High Speed Engine* (pp50-56) in 1987. As a single unit they are necessarily somewhat restricted in their use, but Sir Topham Hatt has been delighted with them and considers their restriction a price worth paying for the services they can offer.

Daisy (D1)

Daisy is a Metro-Cammell Diesel Mechanical single car unit. Having been built specifically to help on the Ffarquhar branch, she was extremely cocky when she arrived in 1960 – see Branch Line Engines – but after a while realised that she was supposed to be part of a team, and sobered down considerably, to everyone's benefit. She still thinks her ideas are better than most other people's, but now is a little more cautious about saying so!

Boco (D2)

Boco is one of the Metropolitan Vickers Diesel Electric Type 2 locomotives introduced to BR in 1958, having a two-axled bogie (Bo) at one end and a three-axled bogie (Co) at the other. During its British Railways life this was not a greatly successful type: the engines worked mainly in the Barrow area, and the Fat Controller, seeing them, decided what he thought was wrong with them and worked out how he might put it right. He did and Boco has fully justified his confidence. He is used on all sorts of duties and is truly, as The Fat Controller remarks in *James and the Diesel Engines* (p8) a 'versatile' engine. One of the class (D5705) has survived and is undergoing restoration at the East Lancashire Railway.

Bear (D3)

Bear is an ex-BR Western Region Diesel Hydraulic BoBo locomotive, of a type often described as 'Hymeks'. His BR number was 7101, and as the Fat Controller acquired him, on approval, in 1967 along with a 'Peak' Type 4, D199 – the Hymek was retained and because of his growl, was nicknamed 'Bear' by the other engines. Like Boco he has proved a worthwhile acquisition.

Mavis

Though Mavis is not strictly owned by the North Western Railway, this seems the logical place to include a note about her. She is a Drewry Class 04 0-6-0 diesel shunter who actually belongs to the Ffarquhar Quarry Company. Her basic work is up in the quarry, but (ref *Tramway Engines* p56) she managed to get an agreement to go down to Ffarquhar station occasionally, an arrangement which undoubtedly suits both parties. Like Daisy, she has her own ideas about things (particularly trucks) and the two of them like nothing better than the chance for a good gossip. Several locomotives of this type have been preserved.

Bill/Ben

Again, these two engines are not part of The Fat Controller's 'family' but it would be unforgivable to leave them out: they are actually owned by the Sodor China Clay, the Company which extracts that commodity from pits about seven miles from Brendam and are 0-4-0 saddle-tank engines with specially cut-down cabs so that they can work through low bridges on their route. Both their prototypes have been preserved – *Judy* and *Alfred* can be seen at the Bodmin Steam Railway.

Visitors

City of Truro

City of Truro visited from the National Railway Museum on a railtour (ref: *Duck and the Diesel Engine* p6 et seq) very much to Duck's delight – he talked Great Western for days afterwards and all the other engines became heartily sick of it! *City of Truro* may be found at the Museum of the Great Western Railway in Swindon.

Flying Scotsman

The Fat Controller arranged for a visit from *Flying Scotsman* – then privately owned – as a treat for Gordon, who had become very depressed at the state of things he was hearing about and seeing on the Other Railway. *Flying Scotsman*, at the time of the story was written, had two tenders, which sparked off a certain amount of needless jealousy in Henry – (ref: *Enterprising Engines*, p12). *Flying Scotsman* may now be found at the National Railway Museum unless engaged on railtour duties.

Stepney

Stepney was a visitor for Thomas from the Bluebell Railway. He thoroughly enjoyed his stay on the Island, during which time he worked on Thomas's branch line, and one gets the feeling that it was only the thought of his responsibilities at Sheffield Park that finally dragged him back home. The Bluebell Railway in Sussex is where he can regularly be found.

Wilbert

Wilbert was a rather different visitor. He is an Austerity 0-6-0 saddle-tank: the Fat Controller felt he needed an engine which was small but powerful to give extra assistance on the Arlesburgh branch (or indeed elsewhere) at busy times and he persuaded the Dean Forest Railway to lend him *Wilbert* for trial. Wilbert spent some time on the Island and like *Stepney,* thoroughly enjoyed it, before returning to his home in the Forest. He has recently undergone an extensive overhaul.

Old Stuck-Up

This is, in fact, a nickname given to a visiting Class 40 diesel (No.40125) in 1984, when the visitor made himself very unpleasant. I think it can be safely said, that unlike the others, he did **not** enjoy his visit to the Island of Sodor, but he had no-one other than himself to blame.

Diesel

Diesel ('Evil Diesel' is a publisher's invention not used in the Railway Series) was, the Fat Controller later acknowledged, not one of his better ideas. He had borrowed a Class 08 0-6-0 shunter (ref: *Duck and the Diesel Engine* p20 et seq) to help in the yard; though welcomed at first he soon made himself unpopular. To get his own back on Duck he made up insulting stories and blamed Duck for them – fortunately the Fat Controller was wise to this and sent him away in disgrace.

Narrow Gauge

Skarloey Railway – 2 feet 3 inches

Taken in number order – the engines are:-

Skarloey (1)

Built in 1865 at the same time as the Talyllyn Railway's No.1 at Fletcher Jennings, Whitehaven, and delivered to the new railway in the following year. The engine arrived cabless as a 0-4-0 saddletank, but after he had precipitated the Manager into a bush on Opening Day (ref: *Very Old Engines*, p26) was given not only an extra pair of wheels to make him a 0-4-2, but a cab as well. A heavy repair was undertaken at Whitehaven in 1897, but nothing further was done and by 1945 he was fit only for steam in extreme emergency – as indeed happened in 1952 – see Old Faithful (*Four Little Engines* p50 and following). Subsequent overhauls in 1958 and 1985 have rejuvenated him.

Rheneas (2)

A 0-4-0 well tank engine, built by Fletcher Jennings to the same design as the Talyllyn's No.2 in 1866. Also delivered cabless he was less used after *Skarloey* acquired his, and also because his long wheelbase was being rather hard on the track. Like *Dolgoch* on the Talyllyn Railway he enjoys 'peculiar motion' which has not made life any easier for the workshop staff. *Rheneas* was overhauled at Crovan's Gate in 1937 and 1943 and in *Skarloey's* extremity became the mainstay of the railway. A heavy overhaul in England in 1961 put him back into fettle, and the works at Crovan's Gate carried out another overhaul in 2002.

Sir Handel (3)

Built for the Mid Sodor Railway by the Falcon Works in Loughborough and, as a 0-4-0 saddletank engine, delivered by sea to Arlesburgh in 1904 to replace a scrapped engine – the MSR gave him blue paint and named him *Falcon*. In 1910 he was sent back to Loughborough, where the addition of a pair of trailing wheels made him a 0-4-2 and much steadier. With No.4 he was sold to the Sodor Aluminium Company on the closure of the MSR and in 1950 bought by the Skarloey Railway, which named him *Sir Handel* after Sir Handel Brown – see people. Wider wheeltreads were provided to cure a propensity for falling between the rails, and he spent the years 1982/4 on loan to the Talyllyn. A similar locomotive has recently been built for the Corris Railway.

Peter Sam (4)

Built in 1920 and delivered by rail to Cronk, Peter Sam is a 0-4-2 saddletank to his builder's (Kerr Stuart) standard industrial pattern. He too was built for the Mid Sodor Railway, where his livery was green and, following the pattern of the MSR's naming their engines after their builders, he became *Stuart*. Like *Sir Handel* he came to the Skarloey by way of the Sodor Aluminium Company and was named after Peter Sam the Thin Controller. An accident in 1961 (ref: *Gallant Old Engine*, p8) allowed an experiment with a Giesl ejector, though unlike the Talyllyn example on *Edward Thomas,* his is still in use. He spent much of the 1990s on loan to the Talyllyn. A similar locomotive has recently been built for the Corris Railway.

Rusty (5)

The Skarloey Railway's 'man of all work'. *Rusty* is a 0-4-0 diesel/mechanical engine bought from Ruston & Hornsby – hence the name – of Lincoln in 1957. He is used for maintenance work and as motive power in a case of emergency or breakdown.

Duncan (6)

Duncan came to the Skarloey Railway second-hand through Sir Handel Brown in 1958 – he is a well-tank built by the Kilmarnock firm of Andrew Barclay in 1928. Increasing traffic was proving too much for the two ex-MSR locomotives to cope with and *Duncan* was brought in to help. Coming from an industrial background he is, as he has been known to say "...a plain, blunt engine." and he is inclined to feel aggrieved about very little at times, but his heart in in the right place. Like *Sir Handel* and *Peter Sam* he has enjoyed a spell at the Talyllyn Railway.

Ivo Hugh (7)

A powerful 0-4-2 locomotive who made his debut in 1996 and has done sterling work for the railway ever since. The heavier work was done at the Fat Controller's works in Crovan's Gate, but he was actually constructed by the Skarloey Railway's own engineering department. His similarity to the Talyllyn Railway's No.7 is explained by the fact that much expertise was passed on by that company in the light of experience with its own engine, *Tom Rolt*, and the co-operation saved much heart-searching at Crovan's Gate. Ivo Hugh is unique in the Skarloey roster as being a side-tank engine, and he is strong enough to handle the heaviest work.

Duke (8)

Duke also came from the Mid Sodor Railway, having first arrived there for its opening in 1880. He was built at Boston Lodge by the Festiniog Railway for the Earl of Sodor, and is a 0-4-0 tender/saddletank engine to a design of George England, of which *Prince* is an example still at work on the Festiniog Railway. In traffic until the MSR closed in 1947 he was sheeted up in Arlesdale shed until discovered in 1969 by the Fat Clergyman – see Sleeping Beauty (ref: *Duke the Lost Engine*, p50). He was overhauled at Crovan's Gate and now runs in his original MSR brown livery.

Fred (9)

This locomotive has so far had only a passing mention, in Story 1 of *New Little Engine* (Bk 40). He is a Hunslet 0-4-0 diesel engine built for work in mines and came to the Skarloey Railway in 1989 from the National Coal Board as a back-up for *Rusty*. The Skarloey bought two engines and made one good one out of the pair; Fred is the result. With a maximum speed under 9mph he is used exclusively for engineering work.

Arlesdale Railway – 15 inches

(NB – similar engines to all of these can be found at the Ravenglass & Eksdale Railway in Cumbria)

Bert

Bert is a 0-8-2 tender engine, who was rebuilt from an earlier 0-8-0 by the Yorkshire Engine Company, and his running gear is not dissimilar to locomotives used by Sir Arthur Heywood on his Duffield Bank Railway. In an attempt for counter poor steaming a pair of trailing wheels was added so that a larger firebox could be inserted, but the problem was not solved until 1973 when a Kylchap blastpipe and longer chimney were fitted. His livery is blue, lined with red. His equivalent at Ravenglass is *River Irt.*

Jock

Jock is a 2-6-2 tender engine built, apart from boiler, firebox and cylinders, at Arlesburgh in 1976, having also been designed 'in house' by Ivan Ferrier the line's CME, working with Ian Smith of the Ravenglass & Eskdale Railway. The design includes the best features of the other three steam engines on the railway. His livery, a pale yellowish green lined with dark red, reminded *Douglas* of the Highland Railway locomotives he had known during his Scottish days; the name Jock was suggested by him and stuck (ref: *Jock the New Engine*, p44). Jock's *alter ego* in Cumbria is *Northern Rock.*

Mike

Mike is a 2-8-2 tender engine who was constructed by Clarkson's of York. The designs attempted to improve on the Ravenglass line's *River Esk*, and, like their own *River Mite*, appears to have succeeded, for he is a tough and strong locomotive. Though thoroughly reliable on the whole he nevertheless, like most of us, has his moments! His livery is red with blue lining.

Rex

Rex is a 2-8-2 tender engine. He is based on a Henry Greenly design and was built by Davey Paxman in Colchester in 1923, at the same time as *River Esk* was being built for the Ravenglass & Eskdale Railway. The engines' lives seem to have run in parallel, for by a remarkable coincidence he went to the Yorkshire Engine Company for a rebuild at the same time as did *River Esk*. The fitting of Walschaert's valve gear solved the problems of both, and although Rex has a penchant for slipping except on light loads he has proved himself, in The Fat Controller's phrase, a Really Useful Engine. He has a green livery with red lining.

Frank

A shunter, painted grey and red, Frank is used for maintenance work and empty carriage movements. He was constructed at Arlesdale out of bits and pieces from other engines, and made his debut in 1990. He is powered by a Perkins diesel engine and is named after the founder of that firm, *Perkins* in Ravenglass, Frank in Arlesdale.

Culdee Fell Railway – 2ft 7.5in

(Though the Culdee Fell Railway has close affinities with the Snowdon Mountain Railway in North Wales, I do not believe that my father intended any of the engines listed below to be specifically associated with any of the SMR locomotives)

Godred (1)

Numbers 1-5 were built at Winterthur in Switzerland in 1900, and work on the Abt rack system, pinion wheels below the engine engaging with a fixed 'rack' of teeth set between the rails. Godred was the ill-fated engine which had the misfortune to become derailed on opening day – perhaps by a stone lodged in the 'rack'. He was so badly damaged that he was scrapped and never replaced.

Ernest (2) and Wilfred (3)

These two engines were delivered in 1900 but by the time of *Mountain Engines* (Bk 19, 1964) had been superseded by Numbers 6, 7 and 8, and appear only in passing in the stories.

Culdee (4)

Culdee, on the way back from overhaul in Switzerland, halts near the Skarloey Railway shed and acts as narrator for the stories in the book, in some of which he is involved himself.

Shane Dooiney (5)

The last of the first bath of engines. Shane Dooiney is not mentioned in the stories of *Mountain Engines* because at the time of them he was away in Switzerland under overhaul. His was the last overhaul to be carried out there – now the mountain engines make the much less expensive trip to The Fat Controller's works at Crovan's Gate when their overhauls become due.

Lord Harry (6)

Lord Harry reached the railway in March 1962, but his behaviour to begin with was not as good. As a result he was suspended from passenger work (ref: *Mountain Engines* p42) but later redeemed himself with a gallant rescue in appalling weather (ref: *Mountain Engines* p48-55). He was renamed Patrick at the request of the young man he had rescued, and re-instated (ref: *Mountain Engines* p56/7).

Alaric (7) and Eric (8)

These two engines, with Lord Harry, are superheated engines of a more modern design – they arrived in the May and July of 1962 respectively, but are mentioned only in passing and take no part in the *Mountain Engines* stories.

Other railway characters

Annie/Clarabel

These are Thomas's two elderly bogie coaches, given to him for his branch line as a reward for proving himself a Really Useful Engine – (ref: *Thomas the Tank Engine*, p62). Annie can take only passengers, but Clarabel can take "...passengers, luggage and the Guard." They are frequently concerned by Thomas's behaviour, but for all that think the world of him and would stick by him through thick and thin.

Henrietta

Henrietta is Toby's coach. When The Fat Controller invited Toby to the Island he omitted to mention her but Toby brought her just the same and she was made very welcome – after all, the alternative so far as she was concerned was a stationmaster's hen-house and that would never have done! Henrietta is actually a four-wheeler, but a very similar ex-Wisbech & Upwell Tramway bogie coach has recently been restored and can be found on the North Norfolk Railway.

Scruffey

A Private Owner wagon, actually the property of S C Ruffey, and like many such wagons, not kept in the best state of maintenance. Unfortunately he makes the mistake of trying to throw his importance about, and an idea suggested by Toad – see below – means that his bragging comes all too literally apart. One is left with the feeling that the Fat Controller, for all his expressed regret, is neither greatly dismayed nor surprised – see *Oliver the Western Engine*, below.

Toad

A certain type of Great Western brake-van was classified 'Toad' and it is one of these that Oliver is able to liberate to the Island of Sodor along with himself and Isabel – see below. Toad is very protective of Oliver and tries to prevent his falling into error, but also suggests the means by which Scruffey's come-uppance may be achieved.

Isabel

A Great Western auto-coach brought over to the Island with Oliver – she has acquired her name because, as Oliver explains, "...there is a bell on her." Along with Dulcie – see below – her duty is the carriage of passengers along what is officially the Arlesburgh branch but is generally known as 'Duck's Branch line'.

Dulcie

When the Fat Controller re-opened the Arlesburgh branch he already had plans for the passenger traffic and was making plans to acquire an auto-coach – this turned out to be Dulcie. The arrival of Isabel to augment the stock, with Oliver, could not have been better timed.

Alice/Mirabelle

Another two Great Western auto-coaches identical to Isabel but painted in Great Western colours with yellowish cream upper panels and dark chocolate lower panels. They are introduced in *Donald's Duck*.

Ruth/Jemima/Lucy

Four-wheeled carriages built by Brown Marshall in 1866 for the Skarloey Railway at the same time as they were building a similar batch for the Talyllyn Railway – which accounts for the marked similarity between the early rolling stock of the two railways. Their equivalents on the Talyllyn are carriages No. 1, 2 and 3.

Agnes

A four wheeled 3rd class carriage by the Birmingham Carriage Company who built two examples in 1866 for the 2ft 3in gauge, One went to Wales, the other to the Island of Sodor. The Talyllyn example is No.4

Beatrice

The Talyllyn van (No.5) by Brown Marshall was thought to be unique until it was discovered that there was another such vehicle, Beatrice, on the Island of Sodor. As with Ruth, Jemima and Lucy, Beatrice was built as part of the same order, and reached the Skarloey Railway at the same time as her sisters.

Ada/Jane/Mabel

Open four-wheeled carriages acquired as a stop-gap when carriage stock was short and now converted into covered stock. They have so far made few appearances in the saga, the most notable being during the television story in *The Little Old Engine* – see below.

Cora

A small four-wheeled van acquired by The Thin Controller for the Skarloey Railway from the sale after the Mid Sodor Railway was closed. She was used as a Guard's Van at first, but after Millicent's arrival has returned to her original use as a tool van.

Gertrude/Millicent

Bogie-coaches rescued from the Mid Sodor Railway and restored for use on the Skarloey. Millicent has a Guard's compartment, which has allowed Cora to revert to her original use.

Catherine

Culdee's coach on the Culdee Fell Railway, the only named example of nine 56-seater saloons belonging to the railway.

Non-railway Characters

Bertie

The red, single-decker bus makes his debut as an unidentified bus in Thomas, Terence and the Snow – ref: *Tank Engine Thomas Again*, p46. He is named in the next story and makes intermittent appearances thereafter throughout the Series. He is good-hearted, helpful and popular character.

Bulgy

A complete contrast to Bertie, the only thing they have in common being their colour. Bulgy, who appears in one story only – see Oliver the Western Engine, below – is a revolutionary double-decker bus who steals the engines' passengers but ends up as a henhouse after becoming trapped under a bridge. Poetic justice, really!

Bulstrode

No less unpleasant but a sea-going barge rather than a bus. He too makes only the single appearance (quite enough really, you might say) and ends up, literally, on the beach. His one saving grace is that he came as a blessing in disguise to an author desperate for a story at short notice.

Caroline

A veteran car who also takes part in only one story – see Stepney the Bluebell Engine, below – but her contribution to that story is, of course, a valuable and entertaining one.

Harold

Harold, though never intended to be a major character – see Percy the Small Engine – has nevertheless turned into one to the extent that I was asked specifically to include him in two of the stories I wrote in the 1980s for the TV series. One of those became *Thomas and the Missing Christmas Tree* (now out of print) and the other appears in *Thomas Comes Home.*

Terence

The orange tractor made his debut in *Thomas the Tank Engine* and has figured in a number of other stories since. Like Harold he has become a well loved character.

Trevor

Rescued from a scrapyard in Edward the Blue Engine, when he is bought by the Vicar of Wellsworth (see People), Trevor too has featured in several stories since. One would be hard put to it to decide who might win in a popularity poll between Trevor, Terence and Bertie!

Side-tracked

There's been a lot of online speculation about certain characters and their unknown fates, and the only character I can say for certain or comment on for sure is that of Barry. Please also bear in mind that my influence on the Series stopped sometime after 2005, and my last book was written in 2011, and that since then, other Rights Holders have continued to create characters. Therefore I cannot possibly comment on anything after 2005.

Barry

Barry was to be a standard 2 6 2 standard tank engine, and was conceived for a new series of stories that were to be written in 1986 that sadly, due to the popularity of the TV show, meant the publishers had something else in mind for that time. Instead Barry was side-tracked and eventually fell by the wayside. The 'roughs' for these stories were sadly lost, and due to the story idea being part of 'The Railway series' even though unpublished, I am forbidden from writing any future stories I may have had about Barry. So I'm afraid for the fans out there, for the engine that almost was, I can only apologise. But then that does add a certain air of mystery to him...

Characters in the Stories

Sir Topham Hatt (1) (1880-1956)

This gentleman is first mentioned in *The Sad Story of Henry* (The Three Railway Engines, p40) when he appears as the Fat Director. Various suggestions have been made for the original basis of the character and all are wrong: my father had not even met the two main suggestions – Horace May of the Bluebell Railway and the Rev'd Teddy Boston – when the story was created in 1942. He is, in fact, based on no-one in particular, though it is possible that my doctor at the time the story was created, made an unconscious contribution. My father wanted to create a benevolent being who was 'in charge'. My doctor, so far as I was concerned, was 'in charge' of me at the time and it may be that he was of portly aspect. I don't know, and I was never even aware of his name, but perhaps an association of ideas evolved in my father's mind.

My father, perhaps warming to the idea, gives the Fat Director a larger role in *Thomas the Tank Engine*. In 1948, the year in which the third book, *James the Red Engine*, was published, our railways became nationalised as British Railways and Company Directors became, at least so far as railways were concerned, beings of the past. Regional Controllers came in – the North Western Railway, now Region, and the Fat Director, though nominally Nationalised along with the rest were actually permitted to go on in pretty much their old way, and things did not change a great deal, apart from The Fat Director's title being changed to that of The Fat Controller. He became more generally known as Sir Topham Hatt (his actual name) in 1984 with the introduction of the TV series: see also FAQ section, TV/Video.

Sir Topham Hatt was, as plain Mr Topham Hatt, the Engineer in charge of the construction of the Tidmouth, Knapford & Elsbridge Light Railway. When the job was finished he was made Director of the Company, and after the Wellsworth & Suddery Railway was linked with the original line at Knapford, was elected a Director of that Company too, the role in which he first appears – see above. He was created a baronet for his services to the railways of Sodor in 1948. He married Jane, sister of Mr (later Sir) Handel Brown, and retired in 1954 in favour of his son, Charles, whom the board had had no hesitation in electing his successor.

Sir Topham Hatt (2) (1914-1997)

Actually, of course, Sir Charles Topham Hatt. He was The Fat Controller from 1954 to 1984, when he retired in favour of his own son – see below. During his period of office he began improvements to the harbour at Knapford, planned by his father, and re-opened the Arlesburgh branch in 1965/6, being responsible for the construction of the Arlesdale Railway and for establishing the ballast consortium which uses it. He married Amanda Croarie in 1940 and they had two children – Stephen Topham (the current Fat Controller) born in 1941 and Bridget, who was born in 1943. Charles inherited his father's baronetcy in 1956 and died thirteen years after his own retirement.

Sir Topham Hatt (3) (b1941)

Sir Stephen Topham Hatt is mentioned with his sister Bridget in *Toby the Tram Engine*, pp8/15, while on a family holiday in England with his parents and grandfather, Sir Topham Hatt (1). He became the Fat Controller in 1984, succeeding to his father's baronetcy in 1997. In 1970 he had married Helen Margaret, a distant cousin and granddaughter of the Rev'd Nicholas Dreswick, the much-respected historian of the Island of Sodor. They have three children: Richard Topham, born in 1972 and the current Sir Topham Hatt (4), Charles Nicholas (1974) and Emily Helen (1977). He played a part in arranging for the construction of the Arlesdale Railway's new locomotive, Jock, in 1990, a project which has been dear to his father's heart. With great skill he masterminded the arrangements for the royal visit in 1995, when he welcomed the Prince of Wales on his first visit to the Island – ref: *Thomas and the Fat Controller's Engine* pp54/60. After retiring in 2023, and refusing to let his age effect him, he helped setup and became Chairman of the recently constructed Crovan's Gate Preservation Society (CGPS) of which Neil is to be the first working engine of its museum.

The Fat Controller (4) (b1972)

As Heir apparent, Richard Topham Hatt succeeded from his father as The Fat Controller in 2023 who retired at the age of 82. At an age of only 51, the new Fat Controller no doubt has a long and exciting career ahead of him, and everyone on the Island is excited at what the future for the Island of Sodor and its railways holds with Richard now at the helm. One of the Fat Controllers first tasks was to present his father a unique retirement gift, that of Neil, one of the oldest working engines on the Island, to be the first engine entered into the Crovan's Gate Preservation Society.

Sir Handel Brown (1) (1875-1950)

He served as Liberal MP for the Sodor East constituency from 1910 to 1929 and again as a National Liberal from 1931 to 1936 – he was created Baronet in 1937 for "Outstanding Public Service". He bought the failing Crovan's Gate Mining Company in 1909, and though the slate quarries served by the Skarloey Railway (both were included in the sale) failed in 1924 he promised to keep them going until his death. When this occurred in 1950 however, they survived against all odds, thanks to Mr Robert Sam, (see below) Sir Handel's Manager. Sir Handel married Dorothy Lloyd in 1920 and their son, Sir Handel Lloyd, born in 1924, is the Owner of the Skarloey Railway referred to in the books.

Sir Handel Brown (2)

Sir Handel Lloyd Brown is the only son of Sir Handel and Dorothy Brown and the present 'Owner' of the Skarloey Railway. His home is at The Rowans, near Cros-ny-Cuirn (the ford of the mountain ash) and about five miles north of Crovan's Gate. He succeeded to both title and property in 1950, though he had in fact been administering the holding for some 15 years. In 1951 he married Rachael Qualtrough, a descendant of the family of Lancelot Qualtrough, the last Bishop of Sodor. They have two children, Rebecca Dorothy (born 1954) and Handel Qualtrough, born 1957, who has administered the Estate since 1994 but who will not, we hope, succeed to his father's baronetcy for some years to come.

Robert Sam (1881 – 1971)

Mr Robert Sam was Sir Handel Brown's General Manager of the Skarloey Railway, having joined the Company at the age of 16 in 1897. He took over as General Manager in 1936 and for some time before Sir Handel (1)'s death in 1950 he ran the railway with the line's Foreman, Mr David Hugh. This continued for a little while after 1950, until Robert stepped down in favour of his son Peter, The Thin Controller (1).

The Thin Controller (1) (b1915)

Mr Peter Sam was born in 1915, the only son of Robert Sam (see above). Having, like his father, spent his entire working life with the Skarloey Railway, he took over from his father as General Manager in 1951: he is the Thin Controller referred to in all stories except those in *Great Little Engines* and *New Little Engine*, having retired in 1980.

The Thin Controller (2) (b1948)

Peter Sam's son Roger, who had been acting as Assistant Manager since 1970, was unanimously accepted by the Skarloey Railway Board as his father's successor, and has continued to foster the links formed by his father with the Talyllyn Railway in Wales. He was instrumental in persuading the Board that a new engine was required, and personally suggested its name to honour another employee, Ivo Hugh (see below) and the faithful service that he had given to the railway.

Ivo Hugh (Mr Hugh) (b1921)

Ivo Hugh, the son of David Hugh, Sir Handel Brown (1)'s Foreman, joined the railway as a Platelayer/Fitter in 1940. His potential was quickly realised, but it was not until his father retired in 1951 that the chance arrived for him to take over as Foreman in his place. He himself retired in 1991, but still lives beside the line and was able in 1996 to christen the new locomotive with his own name, a very closely guarded secret. His son David, born in 1950, followed his father's footsteps both as Fitter on the railway and as Foreman, a post to which he was promoted in 1991. David is the present 'Mr Hugh' in the stories.

Mrs Kyndley

Mrs Kitty Kyndley lives with her husband in a cottage beside Thomas's branch line, just south of the tunnelmouth. She made her debut in the stories when, though ill and confined to bed, she was able to save a train from collision with a landslide by hanging her red dressing gown out of her bedroom window (ref: *Toby the Tram Engine* p52). She has since received several mentions in passing, having recovered from her illness, and though the purist may doubt her longevity (she was middle-aged in 1952!) it is probable that most references concern events occurring around that time. Though now elderly she is still active, however, and still waves to the trains as they pass.

Jem Cole

Jem Cole makes a single appearance – at least by name – in the stories (ref: *Edward the Blue Engine* pp40/44) as the driver of Trevor the Traction Engine before Trevor was bought by the Vicar of Wellsworth (see below), the Rev'd Charles Laxey. Although not specifically stated, it can be safely assumed that after the purchase the Vicar continued to recruit Jem's services when a drive for Trevor was required.

Tom Tipper

Tom Tipper is a postman who – so far, at any rate – has made but a single appearance in the stories (ref: *Really Useful Engines*, pp22-32). He has retired from the Post Office now and lives a quiet life with his wife in a cottage near Ffarquhar station.

Jeremiah Jobling

Jeremiah Jobling emerges briefly from obscurity when, under protest, he donates one of his leather bootlaces to the repair of a vacuum pipe – *James the Red Engine*, pp28/30. That task completed, he has descended into obscurity once more, wiser, perhaps than before.

The Vicar of Wellsworth (b1920)

The Rev'd Charles Laxey, a cousin of the late Rev'd Peter Dreswick, Vicar of Arlesburgh. in 1954, when he purchased Trevor the Traction Engine from the Wellsworth scrapyard (*Edward the Blue Engine*, p38/46), he was a youngish man with sons of 8 and 6. His final appearance in the Series was in *Thomas and the Twins* p36/46 and shortly after that he retired with his wife to a cottage on the outskirts of Brendam; it stands near the railway, so he is able to maintain his acquaintanceship with Edward and his crew. The elder of the boys followed his father into Holy Orders, and was lucky enough to be offered the living of Wellsworth on his father's retirement, so Trevor still lives at the Vicarage there. Thanks to earlier tuition by Jem Cole (qv), Trevor's current owner has become an able driver and mechanic in his own right. The younger son, after obtaining a First in English at Oxford, joined the publishing firm of Chatter & Windows (still, we are glad to say, unabsorbed into a conglomerate) and has worked his way up to the post of Editorial Manager.

The Refreshment Lady (1906-1986)

The Refreshment Lady continued her work with the Skarloey Railway for some ten years after the incident related in *Four Little Engines*, pp34/48 and then enjoyed 21 years of contented retirement before her death in 1986. Her son-in-law – who was, as a newly-married man, actually the driver of *Peter Sam* on the day in question – is now also retired. He and his wife live near the line in the cottage that the Refreshment Lady left to them in her Will.

The Small Controller (b1936)

This is actually Mr Francis Duncan who is, strictly speaking, General Manager rather than a Controller. He was appointed when the Arlesdale Railway was opened on the trackbed of the Mid Sodor Railway in 1967, and is now approaching a remarkable 40 years of service to the line. Now nearing 70 he is still hale and hearty ("Good for another decade," he laughingly boasts), but he has let it be known that he intends to retire on achieving that landmark. He has never married, preferring to devote his life entirely to the railway, and it is felt in many quarters that the example set in his service to the line may be a difficult one to follow.

The Fat Clergyman (1924-1986)

This character really is based on the Rev'd E R ('Teddy') Boston, as anyone who has recognised his portrait in many of the illustrations in *Small Railway Engines* and *Duke the Lost Engine* will know. He and my father met in the late 1940s, and it was a friendship which grew during the next decade, when my father was Vicar of Emneth, just outside Wisbech and Teddy was curate of St. Peter's, Wisbech. Teddy later established the Cadeby Light Railway in his Vicarage there, a project which, for many years, held regular open days on the first Saturday of each month through the summer. Sadly the railway was closed in May 2005.

The Thin Clergyman (1911-1997)

My father personified himself in this character, and took great delight in relating some of the adventures, suitably adapted, that he had shared with 'The Fat Clergyman' on the Ravenglass & Eskdale Railway over the years. The one exception is the story of the finding of Duke, which, while based on the fact of an engine's discovery buried in the South American jungle, was nothing like so immediate or painful to the Fat Clergyman as the tale might have us believe.

Nancy (b1953)

"Nancy is a Guard's daughter." From the stories we actually know no more about her than that, and that she is the recipient of several of Skarloey's reminiscences. In fact her proper name is (or was at the time) Nancy Rushen, and she is distantly related to the Thin Controller (2), for she is the great-granddaughter of Beatrice, on of Mr Robert Sam's sister. Since the stories were written she has married and gone to live in the Isle of Man with her husband, whom she met while he was working as a volunteer on the Railway. They make the short journey back to Sodor to see their married daughters and the railway as often as they can.

Lizi and Kathy

These two girls are also Guard's daughters as it happens, but they belong to the Talyllyn rather than the Skarloey Railway. Lizi and Kathy Presres (Pr: Pressers) live in Tywyn, the headquarters of the Talyllyn Railway, and are on a holiday visit to the Island of Sodor when they remind Peter Sam of an incident that occurred while he was in Wales – ref: *New Little Engine*, p36.

Signalmen, Stationmasters, Inspectors and other railway officials, far too numerous to mention and sadly neglected as to names, are recorded in the chronicles. They appear, do their duty, pass through and are never heard of again. Without them, of course, the railway could not function, so it is fitting therefore, that they should all have at least a general mention and recognition in these pages.

Your Frequently-Asked Questions Answered

The questions answered below are grouped in five sections for easy reference – Books, Engines, Island of Sodor, Video/TV/Online and General, in that order. The questions themselves do not, however, appear in any particular order within those groups.

Books

***Q* Why can't I buy the whole Railway Series?**

A Because the publishers – Egmont Children's Books – have claimed that falling sales make them commercially unviable. But if they aren't there for people to buy in the first place no one can possibly know how viable they are, can they? The complete Series has now been unavailable (At this new time of writing – October 2025) for the best part (or should that be worst?) part of 20 years, and the evidence of my own eyes at bookshops, together with the charity and other sales in which I am involved, suggests that there is actually a wide and eager market for them, which might be tapped to the benefit of everyone. I have a job to keep the few that are available on my sales table, anyway.

***Q* Why does the picture on page 9 of *Tank Engine Thomas Again* depict on the left an engine which looks like Gordon when the text refers to Henry?**

A At the end of Henry's escapade in the tunnel in *The Three Railway Engines*, the Fat Director asked (ref: *Edward, Gordon and Henry*, p60) if he would like a new coat of paint, and suggested blue and red, to which Henry agreed. "Then," he said, "I shall be like Edward." Unfortunately this made him look exactly like Gordon too, and in this picture the artist made the mistake of giving him square buffers like Gordon's. The error has been a source of confusion to generations of children and parents ever since.

***Q* When did the Railway Series start?**

A In 1942, when the author's son Christopher caught measles – for more information see Introduction.

***Q* Where are Gordon's Hill, Henry's Tunnel, Thomas's branch line, etc?**

A These are the questions that started the Island of Sodor off in the first place. All these locations can be found on the map that forms the cover of this book.

***Q* Who or what persuaded your father to publish these stories?**

A It was a 'who' – my mother: see Introduction

***Q* Did your father ever write any stories apart from those to do with Thomas?**

A Yes, he wrote two books for older children about a little red three-wheeled car called Belinda, and later told me that he got the idea when driving past the Reliant works on the A5, on our trips to Wales. *Belinda the Beetle* and *Belinda Beats the Band* were published in 1958 and 1961 respectively, by the Brockhampton Press, and republished in paperback editions with new illustrations in 1992. Though not a story, he also wrote, in 1951, a book of prayers for children called Our Child Begins to Pray.

Q **Is it true that the Railway stories are based on real-life incidents?**

A Certainly – for specific examples see the 'Stories' chapter.

Q **How do you find these 'real-life' ideas? Where do they come from?**

A My father had an extensive library – which I have inherited from him – and he used to subscribe to various magazines which often had little snippets of odd or unusual stories. Ideas often came from the magazines or books, many of which were written by railwaymen or people who had worked for the railway. Then there were newspapers, and he kept scrapbooks – which my son, Richard now has – cuttings and other bits and pieces that his brother or members of the public sent him, odd anecdotes that people told him, and so on.

Q **Why are the 'Thomas' books still popular as ever?**

A There have been as many reasons put forward, almost, as there will be people reading these words! So far as the original stories are concerned, length, with the language and its rhythm are perfectly judged and general entertainment values are high. Illustration also plays an important part and children not only identify with the characters easily but begin also to recognise and appreciate behaviour characteristics. From a parent's point of view, reading, number and colour recognition, with other educational elements, are all gently incorporated in to the stories, and for the child it becomes a pleasurable learning process. Grandparents (and more recently, I suspect, some great-grandparents) who have been brought up on the stories know they are buying a quality product when they do so – more often than not they go for the original texts. Whether the same will be true in 50 years' time of the grandparents brought up on current non-authentic texts remains to be seen.

Q **How many/what languages are Thomas stories available in?**

A Those that I know about or have copies of are:- English, Welsh, Gaelic, Japanese, German, Danish, Swedish, Norwegian, Finnish, Dutch – and American.

Q **Have the stories always had the same illustrator?**

A For the 40 titles in the Railway series we have used six illustrators. The first did not meet with Father's approval, while the second, who was much better but drew only *Thomas the Tank Engine*, could not be traced after the Second War. With *James the Red Engine*, C. Reginald Dalby took over. He was inclined to feel that because they were only children's books – and in his view were probably here today and gone tomorrow – accuracy was of little importance. But Father maintained, not unreasonably, that since he had taken trouble to make the texts authentic the pictures ought to be accurate too. Dalby retired after Book 11 (*Percy the Small Engine*, 1956) and his place was taken by John Kenney. Kenney lived in Leicester and drew from life, visiting Leicester Central station in which to do so. He drew Books 12 (The Eight Famous Engines, 1957) to 17 (Very Old Engines, 1962) inclusive, and then a husband and wife team, Peter and Gunvor

Edwards held the reins until the end of Father's series. Peter, again drawing from life, did the mechanical bits while his wife added the background, and they imbued a new dimension in to the Series. When I took over the writing in 1982 the publishers found Clive Spong for me, who illustrated all of my 16 contributions and several other books as well – Clive has thus actually drawn more of the Railway Series than anyone else. I have also worked with an artist named Ken Stott on a number of TV Spin-off projects. However since the advent of the TV series there is far more work than any one person could cope with and various publishers have recruited other illustrators, some of whom, in my view, come no-where near previously-set high standards.

***Q* Why did your father put faces on the engines?**

A Originally to make them seem a little more human to a sick child. After all, if you are telling a story about a talking engine, logic demands that the child has a way of knowing how he does it. But it wasn't in any case, a new idea – toys dating from, I think the 1870s in the Museum of the Moving Image (MOMI), on the South Bank in London, also have pictures of engines with faces.

***Q* Did your father have it in mind that the stories would be specifically for boys?**

A Only to the extent that I was a boy and the stories were originally for me. By the time he came to write the next two books (James the Red Engine and Tank Engine Thomas Again) he had probably realised – and perhaps hoped, as all writers do – that they might have a wider audience: that may be partly why Thomas's coaches were called Annie and Clarabel.

ENGINES

***Q* Why was Henry given a new shape?**

A Henry was troublesome. He was not the engine that had been ordered in the first place – the Fat Controller had wanted a Robinson 'Atlantic' (4-4-2) of the Great Central Railway but, so the story goes, was fobbed off with a useless Great Northern Railway locomotive built from plans stolen in Doncaster in 1919. These were for an experimental engine, but were thought to be before the new 'Pacific' type (4-6-2) that Gresley was building at the time. Too late the thief realised his mistake and was delighted to offload his disaster on to the first desperate customer who came along – the Fat Controller. That gentleman remembered it with sorrow for the rest of his days! As chance would have it, in 1951 Henry was derailed in an accident in snow at Killdane (*Henry the Green Engine* p26) and the Fat Controller saw his opportunity. Henry was sent to Crewe for rebuilding and came back a different engine. He has given no further trouble.

***Q* Are the engines named after family, friends, etc?**

A No. My father, warned perhaps by the experience of Christopher Robin Milne, avoided this. The names he chose, with one or two minor exceptions, were selected to suit – in his mind – the character he had decided on for the sort of engines he was writing about.

Q **Was Thomas based on a specific engine?**

A Not at first – the stories were simply accompaniment to the toy engine he had made for me. When they were published he knew he wanted authenticity and needed a genuine prototype for the illustrator to base his drawing on. He chose the London Brighton & South Coast Railway's E2 tank engine (see Locomotives), perhaps simply because he had a convenient photograph to hand.

Q **Why is Thomas blue?**

A That is the colour which he painted my original toy engine – stories about that could only have involved a blue engine.

Q **Why is Thomas a "Tank" Engine?**

A The oblong shapes which run along his boiler on either side are tanks in which he stores his water. Perhaps it is worth emphasising the point that Thomas is a tank **engine**, not Thomas the Tank. Thomas the Tank would be a very different sort of machine.

Q **What does SCC stand for on Bill and Ben?**

A Sodor China Clay – see Locomotives.

Q **What does NW on the brake van stand for?**

A North Western – see Chapter 2.

Q **Why are the faces on the back of the Mountain Engines?**

A The Mountain Engines always push their carriages uphill and support them on the way down – this is the only way, then, that they can actually see where they are going. The carriages keep a look out on the way up the mountain.

Q **What was the name of the Austerity engine, and what was his original colour?**

A The Austerity engine was called *Walter* and his colour scheme is black.

Q **You earlier mentioned Barry who was side lined. Can you tell us anymore about what his story would have been?**

A Barry's stories were divided and developed into later stories involving other engines. I'd love to be able to say more, but unfortunately there isn't anything else to say about him.

Q **In Thomas and the Tiger there is an unknown old engine in the background of one of the images that looks similar to James. Can you tell us who he is?**

A He's an old unknown engine whose identity will forever remain a mystery I'm afraid. Perhaps the fans could come up with an interesting story or three about him...

ISLAND OF SODOR

Q **How/when was the Island of Sodor invented?**

A During a visit to the Isle of Man in 1953 – see Chapter 2.

Q **Is the Island of Sodor based on the Isle of Man?**

A No, but it lies between Man and the mainland at Barrow-in-Furness, and many place names on the Island are rooted in the Manx language. The fact that the feature film Thomas and the Magic Railroad, used the Isle of Man for locations was based, I suspect, more on tax breaks than because of any historical significance, though it was, of course, this later feature that was pushed in the publicity.

***Q* Are the railways on the Island based on those on the Isle of Man?**

A No, emphatically not. The first involvement my father had with the railways on Man was when we spent a family holiday there in August 1958, well after the Sodor railways were created. Father may very well have done some research at that time into the matter of place-names and Manx history to add flesh to his history of Sodor, but the railways themselves were not involved. So far as I know there is a not even a railway incident from the Isle of Man on which he based a story.

***Q* Where does the name Sodor come from?**

A Please note, incidentally, that this should be pronounced 'Soedor' with a long 'o'. If Father had not known already (though I suspect he did), this may well be one of the things he investigated during our holiday in 1958. The name is a corruption of the Suddries or South Hebrides, and since this area, with the Isle of Man and part of Northern Ireland, came at the time under the jurisdiction of a single Bishop his title became the Bishop of Sodor and Man. The South Hebrides are now part of the See of Argyll, but the Bishop of Sodor and Man retains his ancient honorific.

***Q* Is there a railway museum or preservation society on the Island?**

A Yes – The recently built Crovan's Gate Preservation Society.

TV/VIDEO/ONLINE

***Q* What did your father think of the videos?**

A The first two stuck close to the original stories and their authenticity and he enjoyed them. After Series 3 the TV people decided that they could create 'better' material for themselves and we both became disillusioned with the crass non-authenticity of some of the storylines.

***Q* Did you or your father meet Ringo Starr?**

A We both did. I met him only once, at the launch of the first TV series, but he visited my father at his home in Stroud once or twice afterwards. They got on very well.

***Q* How did he meet up with Britt Allcroft?**

A One very wet day in 1979 at Sheffield Park on the Bluebell Railway, they were introduced in the restaurant there. Britt told him she thought the stories were 'made to be brought to life', and with extreme reservations at to whether it could be done, he said he was willing to allow her to try.

***Q* Why is the Fat Controller always Sir Topham Hatt on TV and at 'Thomas' events?**

A Purely for 'politically correct' reasons. In my view it is a great pity that Britt Allcroft was coerced by the Americans into using the character's proper name in order to sell her TV product over there. While understanding the reasons why she capitulated, it has meant that the charm of the character is totally lost. To children a name is a name. Everybody has one, and the joke in the name probably goes way over the heads of most – which makes it pretty pointless. But the words 'The Fat Controller', as it must have done to my young mind, summon up an image to a child and one that he/she can relate to and that imagination can play with. If you doubt me, ask your child to describe the next stout person you see going past your house. Much more interesting. And talking of interest, in my five (so far) visits to the USA and Canada I have been asked about the reasons for the change only three times. I gave the above explanation on each occasion; just one of my questioners disagreed with my view, so I cannot feel that down at grass roots the PC movement on this point, even over there, is really as strong as it must have been made out to be.

***Q* Who benefits from all the spin-offs?**

A I have no doubt that, quite rightly, the various manufacturers get their cut, and a percentage also comes to the family and is distributed under the terms of a Trust set up by my father. No doubt the bulk of the income goes to the Rights holder.

GENERAL

***Q* Were your holidays always railway-orientated?**

A Not specifically, at least while we children were young, because my father considered that he had a wife and children to keep happy too!

***Q* Which was your father's favourite engine?**

A He always claimed he did not have one, on the grounds that he regarded the engines as part of his family and that in a family you do not have favourites.

***Q* Who is your favourite engine?**

A Toby – an engine like Toby (see Locomotives) was the first engine I ever footplated, at Great Yarmouth on 30th August 1951, and it was that evening when Father decided that a 'tram' engine would feature in the next book. I was on Toby right from the start, therefore, and am perhaps unique in that my first two footplate experience were both on J70 tram engines; the second was the following Easter when, discovering that the 'trams' were about to be withdrawn, the late 'Teddy' Boston (later to be immortalised as The Fat Clergyman) arranged for Father and me to spend a day with them on the Wisbech & Upwell Tramway.

***Q* Why has Thomas become the most popular character?**

A Eight of the first sixteen stories were about Thomas, and this seems to have established a 'Thomas books' trend for the Series during the 1950s and thereafter, though they have always been officially known as the Railway Series. In fact, since 1949 only 21 original Awdry-generated stories have been written specifically about Thomas. In 1984 Britt Allcroft's first TV series used Thomas as its masthead, and the publishers have since cashed in happily on it: two later titles *Thomas Comes Home* (in which Thomas plays no part except on the final page) and *Thomas and the Fat Controller's Engines* – originally entitled, quite happily right up to the last moment, *The Fat Controller's Engines* – could quite easily have survived without the apparently obligatory 'Thomas'.

***Q* Is there anyone who could take over your role in due course?**

A I'm happily retired now, so I think that question is now irrelevant. Perhaps back in the day there were rumblings about future family involvement, but I no longer have a part to play in how the future of The Railway Series is shaped so there are no shoes left to fill. This isn't a complaint, just a fact. Besides, my son now has his own successful music career. I've helped carry the torch my father passed onto me these past 43 years, but it is now the Rights holder that carries that torch, a torch that has burned these past 80 years and we have to trust that they, the Rights holder can continue to carry this forward.

***Q* How old was your father when he stopped writing?**

A When asked this question in school I generally have to ask whether the questioner means 'writing the engine stories' (as he/she usually does) or if it is an 'altogether' query. He published his last Railway Series book in 1972 and wrote a further single story (Thomas's Christmas Party) for Britt Allcroft's first TV Series – this was published in 1984. There were also two adaptations of earlier stories as picture books. After his 'retirement' from the Railway stories he wrote a variety of things, from railway history to industrial archeological items – the volume already mentioned, The Island of Sodor, its People, History and Railways was a notable one – and he wrote the Foreword of a book of mine published in 1990.

***Q* Was it ever his aim to write about engines from all parts of the country?**

A I don't think it even entered his head; he was much too practical. To do that he would have needed to still be working well beyond 2010 at the rate of more than a book a year!

***Q* Did he read the stories to you?**

A Always. As entertainment when we were children and later as ' guinea-pigs' when he tried them out on us to see if our reactions were what he wanted them to be. He also knew that the stories were, more often than not, read aloud; he knew also that the best way to find out if a story reads well aloud is to do it – and so he did it to us and made his own judgements.

***Q* Did your father realise what it was he was starting?**

A Certainly not at the time he started it all – all he was doing then was trying to amuse a sick child. No doubt thousands of other parents have done the same without the same results. As time went on though he certainly realised it, and he had also discovered some of the consequences by the time he died.

***Q* What were your feelings about having such a famous father?**

A I don't think 'famous' is exactly the word he would have used. In fact he sometimes, in deprecatory jest, passed it off as 'notoriety' but in any case, for us, as a priest he was always in the spotlight to a certain extent. One more angle on this did not, to us, seem to make a whole lot of difference. In short, any 'fame' he may have had went way over our heads – he was simply our father.

The Stories, Their Origins and Location

THE THREE RAILWAY ENGINES, (1945)

Edward's Day Out

A simple story based on the rhyme quoted in the Introduction to his volume. Edward seems to have been in the big shed in Tidmouth "...with five other engines", and it is safe to assume that his journey, probably a local train as far as Wellsworth for no mention is made of his climbing Gordon's Hill, begins from there. We must remember, however, that at this point there was no Island of Sodor and none of the geography that has appeared since.

Edward and Gordon

Gordon stalls with his goods train on what later became known as Gordon's Hill, which lies between Wellsworth and Cronk – but if Edward lives at and works Tidmouth, how come he is available shunting at Wellsworth to be able to supply banking assistance...? There is no implication in the story that he has had to travel anywhere to find his trucks – but see the comment above about the lack of geography at this stage. The story itself is based on a tale Father no doubt heard from railwaymen at out local station at the time, King's Norton, of similar difficulties experienced by trains on the nearby Lickey Incline.

The Sad Story of Henry

Chapter and verse are not available to me for the origin of this one, though I remember hearing Father tell me how an engine, during the pioneering days in America, broke down in a tunnel and was simply abandoned. The rhyme that opens the story my father recalled form his childhood – a version of it was published in a children's book of verses in 1902, along with an illustration which gave the engine concerned rudimentary human features. Henry's Tunnel lies between Vicarstown and Crovan's Gate.

Edward, Gordon and Henry

Edmund Ward, who published this book in May 1945, requested, on seeing the first three stories, a fourth which "...brings Henry out of his tunnel and gives us a happy ending." This is the story which Father devised for him – Gordon, pulling the Express, breaks down outside the tunnel, and Henry and Edward together save the day.

THOMAS THE TANK ENGINE, (1946)

Thomas and Gordon

Thomas, as station pilot at Vicarstown, cheeks Gordon but accidentally gets his come-uppance when, having taken the coaches of the Express to the platform, the station staff forget to uncouple him and he gets pulled along with the train. I understand that the basis of this idea was an incident which took place at Liverpool Street, London, and the train in question was one of the Great Eastern Railway's 'Jazz' commuter trains.

Thomas's Train

Thomas, agitating to pull a train of his own, gets the chance when Henry is ill but sets off by himself when, in a reversal of the previous story, the station staff forget to couple him to it. Something like this, I believe, also happened on the 'Jazz' service, but has probably occurred elsewhere on other occasions too.

Thomas and the Trucks

Edward visits Vicarstown with a goods train and offers to do Thomas's work while he (Thomas) takes Edward's trucks home. There is another inconsistency here, because 'home' in this case seems to be Wellsworth at the foot of Gordon's Hill, though it would fit with Edward, in Edward and Gordon – see above – shunting at Wellsworth. Anyhow, Thomas here is pushed down the hill by the trucks and is greeted by The Fat Director, who is stern at first, but mellows later. This story brings out some of the dangers involved in working unbraked goods wagons down hills, an unavoidable part of any goods crew's life. It is also, incidentally, notable for the first use in the Series of the catchphrase 'Really Useful Engine'.

Thomas and the Breakdown Train

James, too, is pushed down Gordon's Hill by trucks, and is derailed near Crosby. Thomas is pressed into service to take the breakdown train to the rescue: as a reward for his day's work he is proclaimed a Really Useful Engine and given a branch line of his own along with two coaches. There is no particular incident as a basis for this story, but it does work into the narrative the facts that locomotives once had wooden brakeblocks and that these could be unreliable.

JAMES THE RED ENGINE, (1948)

After a break in writing during 1946/7 while Father was extra-busy sorting out the wartime problems of a new parish, Edmund Ward asked for new stories at about Easter 1948. James was written quickly and, because of this, was always Father's least favourite book, the one that every author will recognise as "...the one he'd like to do again."

James and the Top-Hat

James, a new engine introduced in the previous story, has an outing with Edward on a local stopping train. While standing at Cronk, James, in his enthusiasm, lets off steam and sprays water over The Fat Controller's (ex-Fat Director – see People, Sir Topham Hatt 1) top-hat. That gentleman is cross, and threatens to take away James's smart red coat. Many people standing on a platform near a steam engine must have had a similar experience though, perhaps fortunately, we do not all wear top-hats.

James and the Boot-lace

James, bumping his coaches crossly, causes a hole to develop in the vacuum brake pipe, which brings his train to an un-scheduled stop near Kellsthorpe Road. The leak is stopped with newspapers and a leather boot-lace in an echo of a snippet which my father no doubt read in the pages of *The Railway Magazine* or *The Railway Gazette*.

Troublesome Trucks

There have been many recorded instances of goods trains' couplings parting on hills, and James is only one of a long line of engines to whom it has happened. It happens, inevitably, on Gordon's Hill, but James' eventual success in bringing his complete train home (again to Wellsworth judging by the illustration) also brings a rapprochement with the Fat Controller, who tells him "...now you deserve to keep your red coat."

James and the Express

Gordon, full of his own importance, sets out from Tidmouth with the Express, but a signalman's error sends him round the loop and back to Tidmouth; there is, in fact, no such loop shown on the map, but the story is pre-geography (see above). There have been misdirected trains since railways began, and no doubt Father used this idea as a basis for his story. James, the only engine available, pulls the Express instead and has another success.

TANK ENGINE THOMAS AGAIN, (1949)

Thomas and the Guard

Thomas has his branch line (see Thomas and the Breakdown Train, above), which runs from Knapford Junction to Ffarquhar, and two coaches, whom he has called Annie and Clarabel. This is a simple story of a Guard who gets left behind at Knapford Junction after falling over parcels and being too late to get into his van. More than one Guard has been left standing on the platform, but the particular incident on which Father drew took place at Eastbourne – the Guard involved at that time solved his dilemma by taking a taxi to Polegate, where his train had been held for him.

Thomas goes Fishing

This was a favourite story of my father's (and mine too, for that matter). The water stand pipe at Elsbridge is faulty, so Thomas gets water from the river Els, but fish are included in the delivery and block the inlet pipe to his boiler. The story is based on an anecdote related in one of David L Smith's books about the Glasgow and South Western Railway, concerning a driver who kept fish in his engine's watertank in order, he claimed, to keep the water clean. Incidentally, the bridge depicted in the picture on p19 is based on Brunel's flattened-arch masterpiece across the Thames at Maidenhead.

Thomas, Terence and the Snow

Tales of engines being snowed in are legion, and it is not beyond the realm of possibility that a tractor has come to the rescue on more than one occasion, though it may be that Father read of a specific incident to inspire the story. The tunnel depicted is towards the northern end of Thomas's branch line and the story marks the introduction to the saga of both Terence and a (then) un-named bus, of whom we hear more in the next story...

Thomas and Bertie

...which grew from a board game which my father devised to amuse his three children during a wet holiday in Wales. The game featured an un-named bus and an un-named engine, but these became Bertie and Thomas respectively when Father recognised the race's story potential. The 'top station' refered to is Ffarquhar. There have now been several 'race' stories in the saga, and this is the first of them: I find it a particularly effective story to read aloud, though this comment could be made of all four tales in this book.

TROUBLESOME ENGINES, (1950)

Staff unrest on British Railways was rife when his book was published (1950) and this is reflected in the stories.

Henry and the Elephant

Father ventured overseas for the second time for the basis of this story, adapting an incident which occurred in India. Of course, substantial adaptation – the elephant becomes a circus animal rather than a wild one, for instance – was necessary, but the fact that the animal was found to be blocking a tunnel, and moved only when prompted by a train is authentic. More importantly for the tone of the book, it gives Henry a grievance, as does...

Tenders and Turntables

...with regard to Gordon and James respectively. Gordon jams the turntable at Tidmouth and cannot be turned (an everyday railway occurrence), and so has to pull his next train backwards. When it is James's turn he is blown round like a roundabout, as was a locomotive in a famous incident at Hawes Junction, and the three engines decide to go on strike in protest. That turntable from Hawes Junction, incidentally is now at Keighley, Yorkshire, and is used to turn the locomotives of the Keighley & Worth Railway.

Trouble in the Shed

The shed in the title is at Tidmouth and the Fat Controller is not amused. He tells Edward to shunt for the big engines for the time being, but then buys Percy to do this work while Thomas and Edward run the trains – the strikers are the subject of a 'lock-in'. Percy proves great success, and has become one of the more popular engines with children. Though I haven't counted there must be almost as many stories in the saga about him as there are about Thomas!

Percy Runs away

And this is another of them. Percy, while shunting, finds himself stranded on the main line in front of Gordon, approaching at speed with the Express, a story which I know to be based on fact, though my father's record of the incident and the original location has disappeared. The story's location on the Island is at Knapford Junction, and Percy reaches Wellsworth before he is finally turned off the main line. In the omission by the engine-crew to carry out Rule 55 at Knapford Junction this incident too reflects a real one at Hawes Junction in 1910 though, thankfully, with less tragic results.

HENRY THE GREEN ENGINE, (1951)

Coal

Henry is in a bad way. As explained above (see Locomotives), he is not the engine the Fat Controller had wanted and his firebox is too small for the work he is required to do. My father was minded to write him out of the Series altogether, but realised what an uproar that would cause from the Henry fans, and this book represents a rethink, creating causality for the Fat Controller to keep him. In this story special Welsh coal is bought for Henry as an experiment, and proves that Henry can make the steam he needs, given the proper conditions.

The Flying Kipper

Father's solution to Henry's problem was an accident, which takes place at Killdane, beyond the top of Gordon's Hill, while Henry is hauling the nightly fish train, 'The Flying Kipper', to the mainland. The situation is reminiscent, though not exactly described, of the accident at Abbot's Ripton in 1876, when ice and snow caused a signal failure and collision. Henry is sent away to Crewe for a rebuild and, because William Stanier, now in charge at Crewe, owes Sir Topham a favour, Henry comes back looking not unlike one of Stanier Class 5MT locomotives. Bad steaming has never caused trouble since.

Gordon's Whistle

Gordon is upset by Henry's cheerful whistling, and makes reproving remarks about it. But the other engines have the last laugh when Gordon's whistle jams open and has to be righted with hammers. This sort of mishap was fairly frequent on the real railway, and I witnessed something similar myself on the preserved Talyllyn Railway during the summer of 2004.

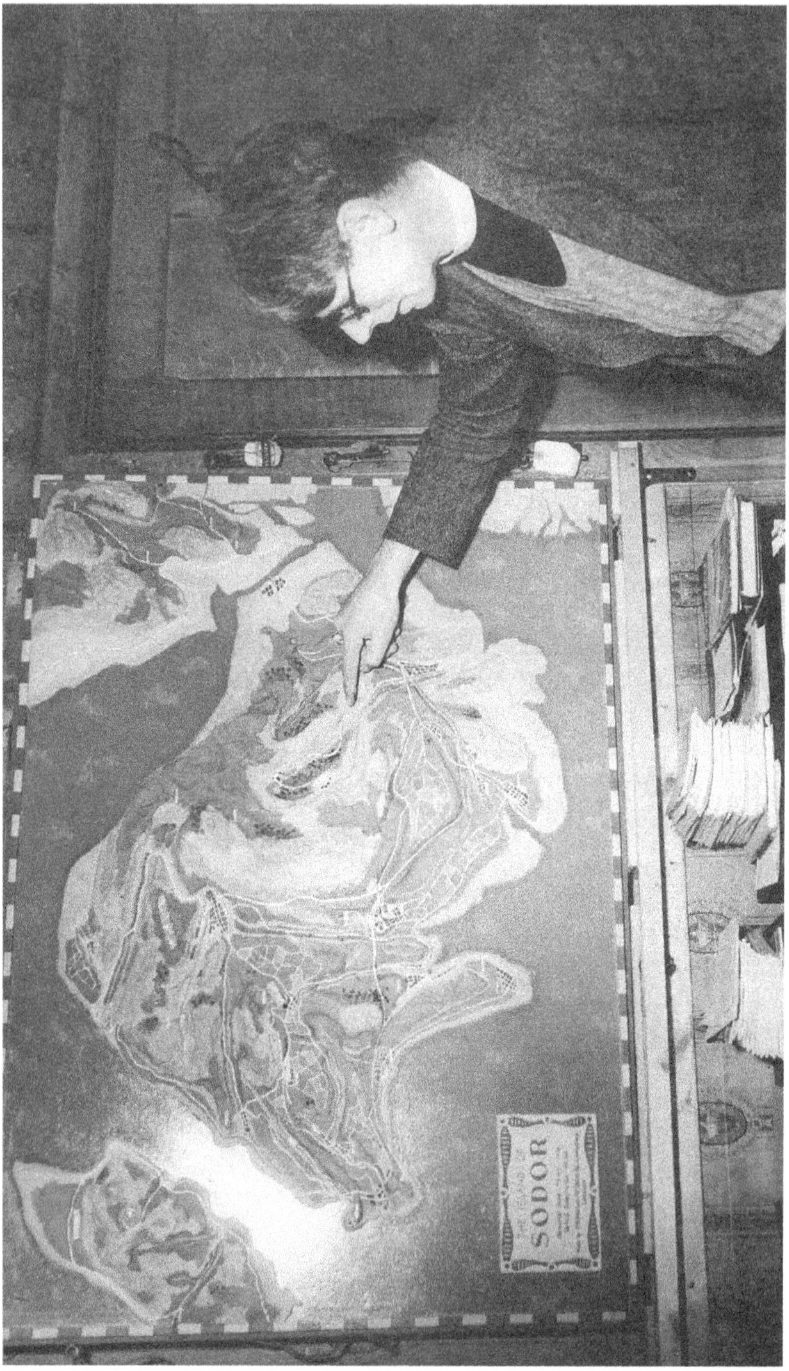

The Rev W Awdry in his study at Emneth, 1955, with the relief map of the Island of sodor which hung on his wall. He is indicating the course of the Skarloey Railway. (Wisbech Advertiser)

Left: three generations of Awdrys at Christmas 1991 - Christopher (top), WVA (centre) and Richard, then aged 11 (Alan Mott)

Below: early models built by WVA and photographed in 1953 - from right, Thomas (1948), Annie (1926/7) and Clarabel (1948). These models ran on several version of the 'Ffarquhar branch'. (Wisbech Advertiser)

Above: The original 'Thomas', with such rolling stock as survived in 1990. The engine was made for the author late in 1942 and the rolling stock during the two or three years following. (Alan Mott).

Below: the author with a group of youngsters during a literacy class, part of a 'Learning with Thomas' fortnight at the Kent & East Sussex Railway in June 2002. (Helen Awdry)

Above: the author ringing the Sleaford Town Crier's bell to start a Blue Peter Bikeathon for Leukaemia Research at Spalding on 11th May 2003. (Andy Fuller)

Right: Jasper, Alberta, Canada, 15th May 2004. From the left Ray Smalley (Thomas merchandising agent), Ross Pugh (Jasper Camera and Gift), Thomas and the author relax for a moment during an event at Ross Pugh's store. (Helen Awdry)

Above: the author in 2019 enjoying a cold winter's day out on the water on the South Coast of England.

Right: The author and his wife, Helen in 2016 visiting the Watercress Line in New Alresford. (Helen Awdry)

Percy and the Trousers

This story, as Father acknowledges in print, is based on one told by his friend C Hamilton Ellis in *The Trains We Loved*. Percy wants a scarf, but acquires one he would rather not have had, when, coming quietly into Tidmouth station, he hits a luggage trolley and gets The Fat Controller's trousers wound round his funnel. This is the shortest story in the Series (only 4 pages) and Father consequently managed to squeeze five stories into this book, making it unique in that respect.

Henry's Sneeze

Vandals who drop things on engines were, alas, just as rife in 1951 as in present day. From a bridge near Crosby boys drop stones on Henry and his driver decides to use a steam engine's ability to emit soot and ash from its funnel on demand to punish them – the process, possible with an engine fitted with an ash ejector, was described in The Railway Gazette c 1960. The originally published text of the story referred to the boys running away "...as black as ni**ers..." but the book had been in print for some years before anyone thought that the phrase might cause offence. As a result the passage now, quite rightly, refers to 'soot' instead.

TOBY THE TRAM ENGINE, (1952)

My father, accompanied by myself, saw his first 'tram' engine on 30th August 1951, on the fishquay at Great Yarmouth, and it was there that the idea for this book germinated.

Toby and the Stout Gentleman

While much Toby material was subsequently gleaned from the Wisbech & Upwell Tramway, this is perhaps the place to try to scotch the myth, current in those parts, that their Tramway inspired the book: it was as described above. We did not visit the Tramway at Wisbech until Easter 1952, and by that time all the first Toby stories were done and dusted for publication that autumn. The first story sets the scene, and Toby's line, depicted in a setting quite unlike the Fens, is visited by a Stout Gentleman and his family while on holiday. The line closes but we have a cliffhanger which leads into...

Thomas in Trouble

...when Thomas, running the roadside tramway to the quarry at Ffarquhar, is told by a policeman that he is in breach of the law in the matter of cowcatchers and sideplates. The Fat Controller – who turns out to have been the Stout Gentleman in the previous story –

remembers Toby and brings him and his faithful coach Henrietta to the Island of Sodor to run the tramway instead of Thomas.

Dirty Objects

This is one of my favourite stories. James is boasting how wonderful his paintwork is and how he is never dirty, but as in all these tales, pride comes before a fall – pushed down Gordon's Hill by his trucks, he collides with two tar wagons, becoming "...black from smokebox to cab." Though the location is not specified, this must, since it lies at the foot of Gordon's Hill, take place in the goods yard at Wellsworth, though it is not made clear why Toby, a long way from his roadside tramway, should be there and available to help sort out the mess. The most likely explanation is that he is on the way to Crovan's Gate for an overhaul and happens to be handy at the time.

Mrs Kyndley's Christmas

This story sees Mrs Kyndley's debut in the series. Ill in bed, she spots a landslide in the cutting just below the tunnel on Thomas's branch line and hangs her red dressing-gown (shades of *The Railway Children*) from the window as a warning for the train to stop. It does, and as a 'thankyou' for her services The Fat Controller and the passengers give her a trip to Bournemouth (p62) to recuperate from her illness.

GORDON THE BIG ENGINE, (1953)

Off the Rails

Gordon, whose fire has been sluggish, begins to make steam while he is on the Vicarstown turntable and he runs forward off it to the end up in a ditch – this actually happened at South Lynn, Norfolk, when an engine, 4MT 2-6-0 No. 43142 was being turned to take a train back to Peterborough. The newspaper cutting from which my father took the idea is undated, but my guess would be that the incident occurred around 1950. Even the method adopted to rescue the locomotive is used in the story exactly as it is described in the paper.

Leaves

This episode takes place on Gordon's Hill and is based on an incident which actually took place in Bincombe tunnel, Sussex – in slippery conditions a locomotive was dragged back by the coaches, it was supposedly pulling. Gordon's input to the story of James' predicament is all part of the rehabilitation process following Gordon's disgrace in the first story.

Down the Mine

Thomas, after cheeking Gordon about his adventure in the ditch, gets his own come-uppance when he falls through the roof of a lead mine. This story is based on the incident of 1892, when a Furness Railway engine, at Lindal-in-Furness, was engulfed in a collapsing mineshaft and sank out of sight – it is now reckoned to be around 200 feet underground. I used to use this story in schools to explain to children how an author adapts ideas – obviously if Thomas had gone down the full distance there would have been no more stories about him, so my father instead deliberately arranged a situation in which Thomas went so far and no further. Gordon continues his rehabilitation by hauling Thomas back to firm ground.

Paintpots and Queens

The Island of Sodor has a Royal visit, but who will pull the Royal Train? Henry, in line for the job, upsets a painter at Tidmouth, who falls and drops his paint – this did happen, I believe at Preston – and Gordon gets his reward. I have always thought this story a small masterpiece: one very tiny authentic incident around which is woven an interplay that never loses its drive or interest.

EDWARD THE BLUE ENGINE, (1954)

Cows

There was an occasion in South Africa when a herd of elephants charged a train and did some damage to it. We don't have elephants on the Island of Sodor – except when the circus comes – but my father coupled this idea with a perennial problem here, that of livestock straying on to the line. After teasing Edward about his train, charged by cattle on the main line between Crosby and Wellsworth, it is Gordon himself who is embarrassed when he encounters a wandering cow and her calf on a bridge near Balladrine.

Bertie's Chase

Something like this happened, I think in Ireland – a bus, running late, tried by stages to catch up with a train, and, as Bertie does, eventually succeeded. Bertie starts his chase of Edward's train with Thomas' late arriving passengers from Knapford Junction and, after another abortive effort at Wellsworth, finally catches Edward at Maron, the station near the summit of Gordon's Hill.

Saved From Scrap

This is the story which introduces one of the Series' best-loved characters – Trevor the Traction Engine. Trevor is for sale in a scrapyard at Wellsworth, and Edward persuades the Vicar of Wellsworth (see people) to buy him. The tale was inspired by a clergyman neighbour of Father's, who did precisely what the Vicar in this story does with Trevor.

Old Iron

This story is based on an incident noted in the *Daily Express* and reprinted *The Railway Gazette* around 1954, when the rescue of a runaway engine was achieved, near Alton, Illinois, in the manner described – though I'm not sure that today's Health and Safety Inspectors would approve! James runs away from Maron and is recovered roughly midway between Killdane and Kellsthorpe: it is Edward, of course, who comes to James's rescue, thus earning himself an overhaul.

FOUR LITTLE ENGINES, (1955)

This book was suggested to my father by the then General Manager of the Talyllyn Railway, Tom Rolt, when Father was doing a stint as a volunteer in 1952, as an idea for publicity for the Railway. Subjects for the stories suggested themselves quite quickly and the Skarloey Railway was thus created, though the book itself had to wait until 1955 for publication – see below.

Skarloey Remembers

The publishers gave some resistance to a book about 'new' engines at first, but a compromise that they should be introduced by a well-known engine, gives Edward the role of 'listener' in this introductory tale. Parallels to the Talyllyn are very close – for details of the relationships between the Skarloey engines and the real thing, see Locomotives.

Sir Handel

In his previous life, on the Mid Sodor Railway, Sir Handel was a passenger engine. He objects strongly (and rudely) to four-wheeled coaches and when told to pull trucks settles himself between the rails in pique. Very authentic – when No.3 came from the Corris Railway to the Talyllyn in the early 1950s his wheeltreads were too narrow for the Talyllyn's sometimes rather liberal gauge and he spent some time between the rails!

Peter Sam and the Refreshment Lady

Father loved a story against himself, and I myself can vouch for the authenticity of this one, since I witnessed it from the Guard's Van. Father indeed it was, as Guard, who left the Refreshment Lady behind – a piquant footnote is that the lady's son-in-law was the driver of the train! If pressed to name my favourite story this one comes very near the top of the list.

Old Faithful

There were a number of occasions on which the old Talyllyn engines struggled on in the face of dire adversity in order to keep the trains running, and this story is based on one of them. In 1952, none of us, I think, expected ever to see the old TR No.1 Talyllyn running again, but by 1958 she was, and perhaps, in some small way, this book helped it to happen.

Father was proud of that.

PERCY THE SMALL ENGINE, (1956)

Percy and the Signal

'Backing signals', though they might seem not only illogical but also dangerous, were indeed a part of railway life, and my father makes use of the idea here to land Percy in just the sort of scrape a naive child might get himself into. The signal at which the story takes place is at Knapford.

Duck Takes Charge

One Christmas my father, perhaps tiring of my repeated knocking on his study door to 'borrow an engine, please,' to use on his model railway, bought me one of my own, a second-hand Great Western pannier tank engine. When we tested it we found that one of the wheels was not quite true on its axle so that the engine 'waddled' slightly as it ran – and the nickname Duck was born. Well, he just had to get into a book, didn't he... This story is as imaginary, though, given that the engines are 'human', not impossible one which provides causality for Duck's introduction to the railway.

Percy and Harold

My father found somewhere a note of a 'race' between a helicopter and a train, and again created Harold merely as an incidental character for the story's sake. But, as Father later said, like Topsy, Harold just grew... The new harbour works mentioned in the story are at Knapford.

Percy's Promise

A train was stranded in five feet of water near Hunstanton, Norfolk, after a tidal wave. The crew managed to get the train back to Hunstanton by using the floorboards of the Guard's Van, but there was no helicopter involvement. This was simply the story-teller's evidence of another use for Harold. Harold lives at Toryeck Airfield, beside Thomas's branch line, and the flood was nearby, where the railway runs close to the river Els.

THE EIGHT FAMOUS ENGINES, (1957)

I think my father had half-hoped that, having done a round dozen of books, he could call time on them, so he wrote a set of stories which he considered might round things off. Publishers are generally aware of when they are on to a good thing, however, and an end to the Series was certainly not on their agenda.

Percy Takes the Plunge

I have sometimes wondered whether this story was originally intended for the previous book. I can find in Father's scrapbook no mention of an incident which may have sparked off this story but I have no shadow of doubt something like it happened – it sounds, if you understand me, too good to be untrue! He may have read or heard the tale of the contractor's locomotive which ran off the end of, I think, the jetty at Burnham-on Sea, which I came across only very recently. The harbour in question here is at Knapford.

Gordon Goes Foreign

I suspect an anecdote father was told of confusion between two LMS stations, Euston and St.Pancras (Broad Street was a third) in London may have been the inspiration for this one. Gordon as an ex-LNER engine, would have expected neither, but ends up, to his disgust, at St.Pancras instead of King's Cross.

Double Header

By 1957 we were living near Wisbech and the Wisbech & Upwell Tramway which had used the ex-Great Eastern Railway 'tram' engines. Now and then the 'trams' had to travel to Stratford (London) for repair or overhaul – they had small water-tanks containing only 600 or so gallons of water, and, like Toby, one once found itself stranded and had to be 'helped' by the following train. Toby is heading for the Works at Crovan's Gate, and gets just beyond Killdane when his water gives out and he has to be pushed home by James.

The Fat Controller's Engines

This was to be the final story – maybe. Cavalcades of engines have happened, and something like Thomas's accident certainly did too. I think that the engines' reaction to their adventures is probably exactly right.

DUCK AND THE DIESEL ENGINE, (1958)

Domeless Engines

The Railway has a visit from *City of Truro*, but Gordon takes exception to the fact that he has no dome. The brakeshoe is on the other wheel, however, when, true to a real-life incident, he loses his domecover as its fastenings work loose and wind gets underneath it. This unfortunate (for Gordon) event happens on the viaduct, which crosses the river valley just to the west of Cronk.

Pop Goes the Diesel

I am not sure what it was that encouraged Father to introduce Diesel. They were just beginning to make an appearance on British Railways, and perhaps he felt that altogether too much was being made of them so that they needed to be taken down a peg or two. Diesel, certainly, is too cocksure by half, but he can't take teasing...

Dirty Work

Diesel decides to try and get his own back on Duck, who has annoyed him, by telling untrue stories about Gordon, Henry and James and pretending that Duck is responsible. The Fat Controller, aware of this though the reader is not, sends Duck away so that Diesel can have enough cable with which to choke himself.

A Close Shave

Something like this story happened on the Ravenglass and Eskdale Railway c1960, though on this occasion skilful judgment by the driver enable the two halves of the train to come back together with "...only a slight jolt," according to the newspaper cutting I have. I suspect this idea was combined with a railway-yard collision with a coal-merchant's hut or something similar. Whatever, Duck redeems himself, the Fat Controller reveals all, and Diesel is sent away in disgrace. As to location, the trucks break away at Maron and the barber's shop into which Duck intrudes is at Crosby.

THE LITTLE OLD ENGINE, (1959)

Trucks!

My father took the chance to visit the Skarloey Railway a second time, and used the not infrequent incident of a runaway down a quarry incline to put Peter Sam on the receiving end of a nasty bump and a cold bath. There was a watering point a short distance below the bottom incline on the Talyllyn Railway, which Father used to add verisimilitude to his story.

Home at Last

Skarloey comes home, a story no doubt prompted by the return to the Talyllyn, after overhaul, of Skarloey's twin, Talyllyn. In 1958 a 'new' engine had arrived on the Talyllyn, named Douglas. He becomes Duncan for the Series, and with his short wheelbase and small wheels was very apt to do Rock n' Roll – this story and the next...

Rock n' Roll

...draw on this propensity, which in this particular story is unfortunately only too true to life. As Rusty suggests, however, gradual refurbishment of the track has made this less of a problem.

Little Old Twins

A story which was clearly inspired by a visit to the Talyllyn of a television crew for a programme in which Father took part. The details and the arrangements for the day he witnessed at first hand, and faithfully describes. The story ends with a reference to the Talyllyn and to the fact that 'twin' engines to the Skarloey Railway once existed there.

THE TWIN ENGINES, (1960)

'Hullo Twins!'

Everyone is complaining of overwork. But the Fat Controller has ordered a new engine from Scotland – except there are two! And no-one knows which is which!

The Missing Coach

Donald and Douglas have numbers painted on their tenders, 9 for Donald and 10 for Douglas. One day Thomas cannot find his special coach from his Express. The Twins switch tenders so no-one knows who put Thomas's coach into the siding. Or do they?

Break Van

A spiteful brake van wants to get even with the Twins. One day James runs out of steam on Gordon's Hill, and Douglas is asked to assist. He does it so well that the brake van is demolished between him and the train and the Fat Controller has another dilemma.

The Deputation

The snow comes early that year and the Twins work is splendid with the snowplough. Then Donald rescues Henry and the engines decide to appoint Percy as a deputation to tell the Fat Controller to keep them both. Percy fulfils his role and The Fat Controller agreed with his decision, to great acclaim.

BRANCH LINE ENGINES, (1961)

Thomas comes to Breakfast

One of my father's favourite stories and one of mine too, for that matter. The location is Ffarquhar but whether the runaway on which my father based the story actually collided with a stationmaster's house or some other dwelling I am unsure. I suspect the latter, but the former makes a better story. In fact there was also an ulterior motive behind this tale: the original artist had drawn Thomas with a drop-front to his frame but had omitted to put one on the back – obviously impossible, since this would leave Thomas's buffers at a different height. Father saw his opportunity to damage Thomas's front and bring him back, after repair, with a straight frame – see the illustration on p57 – to correct the buffer levels. The TV image unfortunately perpetuates the incorrect form!

Daisy

Diesel railcars were making incursions on branch lines by 1961, and the Ffarquhar branch is no exception. This is Daisy's introduction and points up some of the problems that there were (and are) with diesel engines at the overload of a fuse or the drop of a trip switch.

Bulls-eyes

Another idea that has probably happened more than once, though there is a note in Father's scrapbook only of a bull that was chased off the line by a farmer and a policeman. Father's solution, I feel, is much more entertaining, though bullseyes as we knew them in my childhood are a thing of the past so perhaps the story is not, perhaps, quite so comprehensible to children (or even some of the parents) of today.

Percy's Predicament

Percy, pushed down the quarry line by trucks, collides with loaded stone trucks in the Ffarquhar yard and ends up perched on one of them. When this story was published, Father had an indignant letter from an ex-railwayman claiming such a situation was not possible. My father had great delight in sending the gentleman a copy of the picture (published in *Model Railway News* in 1958) from which the illustration on p53 was made. For the record, the incident happened at Swanley Junction on 13th April 1876, to London, Chatham & Dover Railway No.123, *Phyllis.*

GALLANT OLD ENGINE, (1962)

Special Funnel

In this first of another set of Skarloey Railway stories, Father combines two ideas: the occasion when No.4 on the Corris Railway collided with a bridge and broke its funnel – the bits, with the collar that held it temporarily together, can be seen in the Corris Railway

Museum at Corris – and the offer of a Giesl ejector to the Talyllyn Railway, which was fitted top ex-Corris No.4. Icicles in tunnels were not uncommon, either.

Steam-roller

Not much doubt where this idea came from, for it acknowledged at the foot of the story's first page – an incident in Ireland related in *Narrow Gauge Album* by the late Pat Whitehouse.

Passengers and Polish

Another of my favourite stories – it reads aloud brilliantly and we frequently enjoy it at Talyllyn Railway 'events'. A similar derailment I witnessed and assisted with on the Talyllyn at Dolgoch during the 1950s, and Duncan's 'strike' is based on an incident when *Douglas* (Talyllyn No.6 and therefore Duncan's alter ego) stalled on Dolgoch Viaduct at a similar sort of period.

Gallant Old Engine

The source of this story is acknowledged too, *Railway Adventure*, by Tom Rolt, the gentleman who started Father off on the Skarloey saga. The Talyllyn Railway's No.2, worn out, shouldered most of the traffic in the early days and, like Rheneas, kept on going on. Without her efforts perhaps the Talyllyn's efforts at preservation might have failed.

STEPNEY THE BLUEBELL ENGINE, (1963)

Bluebells of England

Father, I suspect, held a similar soft spot for the Bluebell Railway in Sussex as he did for the Talyllyn, and I believe this book was written at the suggestion of people connected with the Railway. *Stepney* comes to visit Thomas on the Island of Sodor, and the first story is an introductory one which not only sets out the scene for the rest of the book, but gives a brief introduction to the Bluebell Railway too. The illustrations indicate that most of this story is based at Knapford Junction.

Stepney's Special

This branch line story is based on an incident related in *The Railway Gazette* in June 1959. One night in 1905 a gentleman missed the midnight train to Aylesbury and ordered a special – the 12 o'clock train was shunted at Chorleywood to let the special pass, and the later-running gentleman actually got home long before everyone else...

Train Stops Play

An incident like this happened at Stroud in May 1960, when a train, halting for a signal on an embankment, was asked to move on because it had stopped behind the bowler's arm. On the Island of Sodor the cricket match is at Elsbridge.

Bowled Out

This too is authenticated from the pages of *The Railway Gazette* in late 1960 or early 1961. A new diesel engine, on trial with BR, had to be towed away by a steam locomotive after an inspector's bowler hat was sucked into the fan duct, thus cutting off the supply of air to the engine. On Sodor the incident takes place in Tidmouth yard.

MOUNTAIN ENGINES, (1964)

This too may have been a 'request' book – it is based on the Snowden Mountain Railway in North Wales. I have never felt quite at home with this one – it is out with the normal pattern, but one cannot deny that the stories read well. It may be worth making the point that though 'incidents' at Snowdon may perhaps seem over-frequent, one of the reasons why the book has never had a successor is largely because, since the line is unique in Britain, there are in fact very few authentic incidents on which stories can be based!

Mountain Engine

Culdee, one of the mountain engines, on its way back from repair, halts at Crovan's Gate near the Skarloey Railway, and the opportunity is taken to introduce the mountain railway and explain some of its characters and characteristics.

Bad Look-out

A revisiting of the accident on the opening day of the Snowden Mountain Railway back in 1896, when an engine derails and rolls down the mountain. In Father's version the engine concerned has his parts used as spares, and dumped at the back of the shed, gets smaller and smaller...

Danger Points

Another story based on an actual incident, though rather more recent than 1896. In fact, during the late 1980s and shortly before I was due to visit the library in Llanberis for a session with the local children, there was a second similar mishap. As may be imagined it was the talk of the town though the railway itself was being very stiff-lipped about it. In Father's version Lord Harry, too big for his wheels, disgraces himself by becoming derailed on points at the Summit station.

Devil's Back

Devil's Back has definite affinity with the Clogwyn ridge on Snowdon. Contrary to railway ones, climbing accidents, alas are very frequent on Snowdon, and my father takes the chance to redeem Lord Harry's reputation by having him carry out a brave rescue after one of them. the young man who is rescued requests later that Lord Harry be renamed Patrick after himself.

VERY OLD ENGINES, (1965)

Yet another trip along the Skarloey Railway, but this time we are taken back to the opening of the railway in 1865. This book was to celebrate the Centenary of the Talyllyn in 1965, a fact which provided a very convenient excuse.

Crosspatch

Nancy, a Guard's daughter who appeared in Passengers and Polish (see *Gallant Old Engine*, above), makes another appearance as the recipient of Skarloey's reminiscences about the old days, when he and Rheneas were new to the railway: Father does not miss the chance to get in a mention of another engine like Skarloey, being built at the same time for a certain railway in Wales...

Bucking Bronco

When the Talyllyn's No.1 was delivered it had a propensity to sway up and down as it travelled. My father used this idea, and although Talyllyn did not actually rock anyone off the footplate, the means of solving the up and down motion for Skarloey was the same – a pair of trailing wheels.

Stick-in-the-Mud

Skarloey comes back from repair with a cab as well as trailing wheels, another Talyllyn Railway parallel. Rheneas had not got one and this leads to a certain amount of bad feeling.

Duck and Dukes

For the final tale Father returns to the present day, and the celebrations for the Centenary, as part of which the Duke of Sodor is coming to open the new loop line round the lake. There is a misunderstanding by Peter Sam when Duck, in Great Western mode, refers to 'Dukes' as engines which have been scrapped – though he does not make it clear they are engines rather than people. Peter Sam believes that the Duke who is coming to open the loop line cannot therefore be a real Duke after all, but everyone is mightily relieved when they find that he is! Another reference to the Talyllyn and its own Centenary ends the book.

MAIN LINE ENGINES, (1966)

As Father confesses in his Foreword, Bill and Ben, the China Clay twins came to play a rather larger role in this book than had been originally intended. *Main Line Engines* was the plan and the title, and indeed Gordon, James and Edward are all featured, but the Twins keep popping up...

The Diseasel

This story serves to introduce china clay and the twins, Bill and Ben, (for more details see Locomotives) with a lot of lighthearted backchat around a health slogan in use at the time "Coughs and Sneezes spread diseases – catch them in your handkerchief". The story also brings in BoCo for the first time, one of the only diesels in the saga who never seems to have upset anybody. The 'china clay harbour' is at Brendam.

Buzz Buzz

A swarm of bees escapes at Tidmouth station and James gets stung on the nose. This is based on an incident at London Bridge – related first in the August pages of *The Times,* no less – when staff, passengers and even a train disappeared, as if by magic when just six bees escaped from a damaged hive.

Wrong Road

Over the years a great number of trains have been misdirected for one reason or another – Gordon in James and the Express was one – see *James the Red engine*, above – and Father no doubt had a hard and fast example for this one. The lady in the green floppy hat which is mistaken for the Guard's green flag is authentic too – at Sittingbourne, in 1911. But the Twins' threat to push Gordon into the sea **must** have been Father's fun – mustn't it?

Edward's Exploit

Edward's branch line runs from Cronk to Brendam, and it is during a journey along here that one of his left-hand crank-pins shears, the coupling rod then severely damaging his frame. There was much more serious result when something happened to the crosshead assembly of an express near Settle in 1960. Edward limps bravely home as a single-wheeler, as has probably happened more times on the railway than most of us have had hot dinners.

SMALL RAILWAY ENGINES, (1967)

My father and his great friend the Rev'd 'Teddy' Boston visited the Ravenglass & Eskdale Railway in Cumbria a number of times, and these stories are some of the fruits of their trips – both men are depicted in the illustrations, and in the text are described respectively as the Thin and Fat Clergyman.

Ballast

An introductory story which sets out the causality for the 'new' railway on Sodor, introduces us to the engines Rex, Bert and Mike (for more details see Locomotives) and has a very close affinity with past events on the Ravenglass line.

Tit for Tat

Another example of Father's enjoyment of telling a story against himself, though it was actually poor Teddy Boston who got the soaking, exactly as described in the story.

Mike's Whistle

Something like this, too, occurred during one of their visits, though I confess I do not know whether a cow was involved. Certainly an engine's whistle disappeared into the upper atmosphere.

Useful Railway

The basis for this story is, I suspect, in the 'could have happened' category. A trailer-load of wool-bales falls on the track and Rex collides with them – no doubt someone better versed than I in Ravenglass lore will now write and say, "Yes, this happened at so and so in so and so..." I very much hope they do, but not so far.

ENTERPRISING ENGINES, (1968)

Tenders for Henry

Flying Scotsman comes to visit Tidmouth and Henry is jealous because he has two tender. But he is not so happy when he discovers that the extra tenders he is offered by Duck contain only boiler-sludge.

Super Rescue

This story, as acknowledged in my father's Foreword, is based on an incident which happened to a young correspondent while on a journey to Waterloo in April 1967. A diesel fails and is helped home by Henry – who is also, at least technically, 'failed' because he has lost his regulator.

Escape

I had, until recently, thought this story of Oliver's escape to the Island of Sodor, with railwaymen in the know helping him on his way, to be pure fiction, though the basic idea of preserving locomotives was gathering momentum at the time. Then while I was writing this book, I came across, in a magazine, a photograph of a waybill which, it was said, railwaymen had deliberately altered so that No.71000, *Duke of Gloucester* was sent, not to a scrapyard where it was to be immediately cut up, but to Woodham's Yard in Barry, where it was to languish until rescued. Maybe Father, back in 1967, had heard that tale too.

Little Western

This story is the logical and largely fictional outcome of the previous one – Oliver has escaped. The Fat Controller, unknown to everybody else, actually knows all about the extra engine hidden in the Yard and has arranged to keep him, so all ends happily.

OLIVER THE WESTERN ENGINE, (1969)

The Fat Controller has opened a new branch line, running northwards along the coast from Tidmouth to Arlesburgh, the railhead for the Arlesdale Railway portrayed in *Small Railway Engines* – see above. Oliver, newly acquired, and Duck, with assistance from Donald and Douglas, have been deputed to run it.

Donald's Duck

I confess I have absolutely no idea where the germ of this story came from – perhaps a combination of Duck's name, the Disney character and a bird of some description nesting in an old tender – which is certainly factual. Whatever, it is a splendid opportunity for Duck and Donald to have some fun with a duck-egg. The duck (Dilly) takes up residence at Haultraugh.

Resource and Sagacity

Oliver is getting above himself but is brought – literally – down to earth by ballast trucks who push him into the turntable pit at Arlesburgh. As for the origin of the story, more and better engines have ended up in Oliver's undignified position.

Toad Stands By

Father enjoyed, I think, the pun included in the name given to a particular type of Great Western brake van. Toad is of the old, respectful school, and he and Oliver combine to dispose of Scruffey, a rude and very decrepit Private Owner wagon who is making a nuisance of himself. Many Private Owner wagons were less-maintained that they should have been and I think it highly likely that something similar occurred to such a vehicle.

Bulgy

Bulgy is another of Father's less pleasant characters, who, having tried to steal passengers from the railway under false pretences, gets his come-uppance when he becomes wedged under a railway bridge. It happened in Lewes High Street, *The Evening Standard* told its readers, probably late in 1962, though the bus involved was actually a trolley-bus on a low loader en route to the scrapyard. At least Bulgy did not finish up there.

DUKE THE LOST ENGINE, (1970)

"An engine lost in the South American jungle was found after 30 years. A tree had grown through its chimney and hornets nested in its firebox." The quotation comes from the Foreword to the book, and I am fairly certain that this was the starting point for what follows.

Granpuff

"Granpuff" was the affectionate name by which his young grandchildren knew my father, and his use of it as the title for this story is a good indication that he was proud of it. The story takes us back to the early days of the Mid Sodor Railway, the narrow gauge line from which came Peter Sam and Sir Handel – but their names were Stuart and Falcon then. There was also another engine, older than either of them, called Duke – whom they nicknamed 'Granpuff'. When the line closed Stuart and Falcon were sold, but Duke was put away in a shed and...disappeared.

Bulldog

Falcon – double-heading with Duke, becomes derailed on a rough piece of track – ostensibly through inattention to it – but is held to Duke by his coupling. Duke saves the day by hanging on like a bulldog. There is then a water crisis: something similar happened on the Talyllyn Railway and was solved as described; the old Ealing Comedy *The Titfield Thunderbolt* used the same idea, also drawn from the Talyllyn incident.

You Can't Win

In this story Stuart is called to assist when Duke 'fails'. Duke is not so badly failed as Stuart thinks, however, and visitors, to Stuarts chagrin and Duke's amusement, think that the elderly Duke has been rescuing him! There are overtones of *Super Rescue* here – see above, but in a new setting and with a new slant.

Sleeping Beauty

The Arlesdale Railway – see Chapter 2 – is laid on the trackbed of the Mid Sodor Railway, and the Thin and Fat Clergymen, hearing the Duke's disappearance, set out to find him. The Fat Clergyman does so, accidentally, and Duke is taken away for repair. On the final page of the book he is re-united with Falcon and Stuart, now of course, Sir Handel and Peter Sam, on the Skarloey Railway.

There was no new book in 1971, instead the publishers produced a wallet containing various items connected with the Railway Series – colouring sheets, an information pack, etc. – which they called A Surprise Packet. The Railway Series resumed next year with...

TRAMWAY ENGINES, (1972)

Ghost Train

Father obviously came across a tale of a railway collision involving something carrying lime, and evolved an amusing little ghost story as a result – this goes down very well with children when read aloud. Crowe's Farm Crossing lies between the tunnel and Hackenbeck on Thomas's branch line.

Woolly Bear

I have no doubt of the authenticity of this story, for Father often mentioned it as an example of odd things that could happen – what he failed to mention, at least to me, were the details of the two vital elements of where and when it did happen! Certainly too on the Talyllyn as, I suspect, on many other lines, cutting-side hay was sold to local farmers as a way of slightly improving the bottom line.

Mavis

Mavis is introduced in this story. Drewry diesels like Mavis had run the Wisbech & Upwell Tramway after the steam trams were scrapped from 1953, and by 1972 they had gone too – but see Locomotives. On a frosty day Mavis stops where she cannot restart her train and Toby has to rescue her – the story recalls experiences at what was virtually the only 'hill' on the Wisbech & Upwell Tramway and the embarrassment that could ensue if the driver stopped in the wrong place on a hard winter day.

Toby's Tightrope

I believe that the origin of this story is in America, where a timber trestle virtually disappeared before a horrified driver's eyes! Toby is the unfortunate engine involved here, and Mavis, by helping in his rescue, is able to redeem herself for previous misdemeanours.

This was the final story my father wrote for the Railway Series, though he did write another story, *Thomas's Christmas Party* for the first TV series at the request of Britt Allcroft, which was published in time for Christmas 1984. He also adapted two of his earlier stories – *Thomas Comes to Breakfast* and *Thomas and the Breakdown Train* – as picture books.

Almost exactly ten years after Father's completion of book 26 in the Railway Series I wrote my first 'Thomas' story based on an idea given to me by an engine driver on the Nene Valley Railway. It was begun more as an exercise than because I thought it would be worth anything, but it turned out quite well, so I added three more. Both my father and his publishers thought they were worth more than I did, so in the autumn of 1983 the Series continued with...

REALLY USEFUL ENGINES, (1983)

Stop Thief!

I culled this incident in late 1982 from one of John Thomas's books about Scottish railways, I think the Callander & Oban. The stationmaster at Ffarquhar has had his gardening cups and car stolen. During a subsequent journey Thomas recognises the car, his crew get a message to the police and both cups and car are recovered.

Mind that Bike

Definitely a 'could happen', this one, and I would very much hope it never actually does (or has). Boys are playing with a bicycle on Ffarquhar platform: it runs out of control down the end ramp and, fortunately without anyone on it, disappears beneath Percy's wheels just as he starts away.

Fish

Duck, banking Henry and 'The Flying Kipper', up Gordon's Hill, falls behind the train he is assisting without realising it because the tail-lamp of the fish train has fallen off. Without his banker Henry slows down; in the dark, Duck is unaware of this and when he catches up there is a collision in which Duck is slightly damaged. As here, a missing tail-lamp was responsible for something similiar on the Lickey before the Second World War, though I converted the original common or garden goods train to 'The Flying Kipper' to provide (I hope) added interest.

Triple-Header

The idea for this, my very first Thomas story, was suggested to me by a driver on the Nene Valley Railway, who told of an incident when a 6-wheeled tank engine (incidentally, also named *Thomas*) had, in an emergency, gone to the rescue of a train that was far beyond its normal capacity and run out of steam a mere hundred yards from home. I brought in

Duck and Percy to create a triple-header in which, one by one, each of the engines 'run out of puff'.

JAMES AND THE DIESEL ENGINES, (1984)

Old Stuck-Up

The book's theme, if it can be said to have one, is James's mistrust of diesel engines. A haughty diesel, after spending a night in the steam shed and annoying all the engines, slithers through the end-wall and leaves in disgrace. The idea for this tale came from a photograph in Railway World of a steam engine (actually an A4 'Pacific') peering through the broken end-wall of an engine shed. To change the steam engine to a diesel seemed to add weight to James's attitude.

Crossed Lines

James, while shunting in fog, has a misunderstanding with the signalman and a bogie wagon has one of its bogies diverted along a different track, demolishing a signal in the process. Such diversions are not uncommon, in fact, and nor were mistaken whistles in fog, but the signal was an added extra.

Fire Engine

Henry's tender coupling breaks and, in throwing out his fire, his crew accidentally set alight the sleepers beneath him. I cannot now recall the precise incident that sparked (if that is the right word) this story, but I am assured by those who know – and who, possibly in some cases, had been responsible! – that such a thing has occurred more than once.

Deep Freeze

This too was taken from an authentic incident when, on a very frosty day, a locomotive's tender was filled so full that ice sealed the filler cap and lack of air pressure in the tender caused both injectors to fail. In this story it happens to James who, rescued willy-nilly from his predicament by a diesel (curiously with no identifying marks, though clearly a Class 47), comes to the conclusion that maybe even diesels have their uses.

GREAT LITTLE ENGINES, (1985)

The title of this, my first foray into the world of the Skarloey Railway, echoes that of a marketing group to which many of the Welsh railways belong, the Great Little Trains of Wales. One suspects that only those in the know actually got the point, but I don't think it's actually a bad title anyway. For a few years during the 1980s the Talyllyn Railway 'borrowed' Sir Handel, and these stories make reference to his visit to Wales.

Patience is a Virtue

Sir Handel, at the invitation of the Talyllyn Railway, is asked to go to Wales and gets above himself in consequence. He is sobered down a little when his Guard is left behind because the crowd of passengers in the van, Beatrice, does not give him space to enter. I witnessed the same problem on the Talyllyn during the early days on the Railway.

Peter Sam and the Prickly Problem

Peter Sam boasts that the hedge-trimmings collected on either side of the line can easily be swept aside. He soon finds, however, that when brambles are involved it's not such an easy matter and he has to be cut out of his predicament. This too is taken from an incident which occurred in the early Preservation days of the Talyllyn, and so far as I can judge does not differ much from the original – only the names have been changed...

'Pop' Special

The re-telling of yet another incident excavated from the Talyllyn's past – parties of Scouts gave great assistance to the line in a number of ways during early Preservation times, and this tale tells of a very hot day when liquid refreshment was badly needed and was hard to come by. Duncan's suggestion of a solution makes him the hero of the piece but there are also overtones of the Vale of Rheidol Railway, where there was once a shop purveying such comestibles close to the terminus at the top end of the line.

Sir Handel Comes Home

The title says it all, really, and is a resume of some of the incidents which happened on the Talyllyn during the time Sir Handel was there, complete with an incident just before he left when he ran into a tree at Dolgoch and spent the next day with a bandaged eye. The book is rounded off with a reference to Skarloey's 'twin', Talyllyn.

MORE ABOUT THOMAS THE TANK ENGINE, (1986)

The book for 1986 was already in draft form when it was discovered that Britt Allcroft, anxious to continue with the second TV Series could not, under the terms of her contract, use a set of stories especially written unless they appeared in book form first. The planned book quickly became this one in order to extricate her from her problem and the swiftness of its genesis perhaps accounts for, to my mind, the least effective title in the entire Series – I feel sure we could have thought of something better had we had more time...

Thomas, Percy and the Coal

All the stories in this book take place on Thomas's branch line, mostly at or near Ffarquhar. The general theme is a feud between Thomas and Percy, sparked off in this first tale when Thomas, somewhat unjustly, considers Percy responsible for him (Thomas) getting covered with coal-dust. Incidentally, the incident on which the story is bases happened exactly as described and not in the (improbable) fashion portrayed in the TV series.

The Runaway

Thomas, after repairs, has a stiff handbrake. A relief fireman, not remembering this, thinks it is on, when it is isn't and Thomas, complete with train, runs away from Knapford Junction passing several stations before he is caught by an Inspector. It happened first with one of the 'Jazz' commuter trains out of Liverpool Street, which got some distance along, I think, the Ilford line before an upgrade slowed it sufficiently for someone to hop on board. Ms Allcroft had particularly requested a story with Harold in it, so although not authentic to the original, I was able to oblige since an airfield happens to be conveniently situated beside Thomas's branch line.

Better Late than Never

Delays to trains on the main line because the viaduct is under repair mean Thomas's branch line service is kept waiting so that passengers can keep connections – okay, that's not very authentic to today's Big Railway, but this is the Island of Sodor and the Fat Controller runs trains as a service to his passengers. Thomas's lateness is remarked by Bertie, but then Bertie breaks down himself, and Thomas, running late as usual, is able to come to the rescue of his passengers and take them on to Ffarquhar. This was taken from an incident I read about somewhere, though I'm afraid I cannot now recall exactly where, of a train which was able to help a bus instead of a more usual (these days) *vice versa*.

Drip-Tank

A story which seems to work quite well when read aloud, but about which I nowadays feel slightly uneasy – perhaps because the word 'drip' is no longer current jargon. In the context, however 'wimp' would hardly fit with Thomas's punctured water-tank, so little can now be done about it. Thomas's tank is damaged by a broken coupling-rod, Percy comes to the rescue and the two tank engines make up their differences.

GORDON THE HIGH SPEED ENGINE, (1987)

High Speed Gordon

We have all met Gordon's boasting before, and here, once again, it is about how fast he can go. One frosty morning his train is arranged in such a way that he has to stand outside Tidmouth station – he slips on starting, catches the water in his cylinders and his driver cannot close the regulator. Gordon's wheels go on spinning for 15 minutes and wear grooves in the rails – he slinks away in shamed silence to the shed. Sir William Stanier's 'Princess Coronation' class had a propensity for doing this sort of thing, and as Gordon has a Stanier 'underneath' (see Locomotives) it seemed to me not impossible that he might have inherited the trait.

Smokescreen

Wedding guests at the Bluebell Railway were once (and one hopes it was only once) showered with soot from an engine funnel, and ash thrown from the window is recorded too. Gordon, smarting after his 'spinning' debacle, is trying hard to redeem himself, but all he seems able to do is to incur the Fat Controller's further wrath. He first smothers wedding guests at Wellsworth with soot, while ashes are blown on to the Fat Controller's new top hat at the same place on the return journey. To say that the Fat Controller is not pleased is an understatement.

Fire Escape

Gordon, still anxious to atone for his misdemeanours, loses his firebars while climbing the Hill, and is congratulated for his recovery work but not wholly forgiven for his other mishaps. The actual incident on which the story is based occurred on the Lickey, and the solution given is as described in *Steam Railway* by the fireman who had been involved.

Gordon Proves his Point

Gordon arrives at Barrow, on the Mainland, to find a failed railtour. He is pressed into service – steam is recorded as having substituted for diesel on a Cumbrian Coast Express – his own service back to Tidmouth being taken by a High Speed Train, topped and tailed by Phillipa and Emma – Pip and Emma for short. Pip has failed already (loss of coolant, a recurring problem for HSTs on the Big Railway at this time), and before the journey is done Emma fails too. They are pushed to Tidmouth by James, where they make friends with the others. Gordon, having distinguished himself with the Railtour, comes home next day, is forgiven and all ends happily.

TOBY, TRUCKS AND TROUBLE, (1988)

This title, at No.32 in the Series, was the first not to have the word 'engine' or 'engines' in it. While it seemed a pity that the tradition was broken it became a precedent in that we did not attempt to so restrict ourselves thereafter.

Mavis and the Lorry

The origin of this story, a confrontation between a diesel engine and a lorry, took place on the Wisbech & Upwell Tramway outside the Blacksmith Arms, Elm, on a sharp curve in the road between Wisbech and Downham Market. Here, on the tramway to the quarry above Ffarquhar station, a lorry-driver new to the Island of Sodor is surprised by both the bend in the road and the fact of seeing a train on it – whether the original lorry-driver had the same excuse I have no idea!

Toby's Seaside Holiday

Toby reminisces about the occasion when, in the old days, he was smartened up to go as an 'attraction' at a Festival in a village near the sea on the English east coast. When he gets there those in charge decide he is so smart that he shows their branch line up to disadvantage and he is sent home again. Something similar occurred in connection with a well-known east-coast Music Festival soon after the War – my informant, who is acknowledged in the book, was one of the organisers from the railway side.

Bulstrode

I was very lucky with this story, a simple one about a disagreeable barge who meets his come-uppance when loaded stone trucks run away on the quayside at Knapford Harbour and sink him. My original idea for the third story of this book had failed to come up to scratch and my deadline was fast approaching. The first bit of luck was when I read of the sinking in similar circumstances of a barge when coal trucks ran away at a dock in South Wales – the second lucky break was was that the story 'came' so well that very little revision was needed (almost the only time!) and my deadline was met.

Toby Takes the Road

For this story I used the same bend on Toby's tramway as in Story 1, though in fact the tale I had from the driver concerned occurred at a point on the Wisbech & Upwell Tramway a mile or so nearer Wisbech than the incident in Story 1. Toby's wheels, pushed off the rails by frozen earth, carry straight on instead of taking the curve. The way the driver and firemen got them back on the rails is just as I was told it.

THOMAS AND THE TWINS, (1989)

Scrambled Eggs

Because there are maintenance works on his branch line Thomas is dispatched to help, temporarily, on Edward's branch. At the china clay harbour he encounters Bill and Ben and their teasing in a story involving a change of colour from blue to yellow. The incident with the broken-down lorry, its contents and the result is authentic, but the rest of the tale is down to invention.

What a Picture!

Mr Bill Rogers, a retired driver of the Port of Par engines on which Bill and Ben are based and who helped Father in the preparation of *Main Line Engines* (see above) inspired this story during a visit I made to him at his cottage in St Austell: he had unfortunately, died before he could see the finished version. In fact it combines two of his tales, one involving enthusiasts and photographs and the other a vessel nearly grounded in the harbour and rescued by the engines. On the Island of Sodor the china clay harbour is at Brendam, at the end of Edward's branch line.

Trevor Helps Out

This story takes place near Wellsworth, close to the point at which Edward's branch joins the main line – a similar derailment of goods wagons did actually happen, though one suspects that a traction engine was not so handy to pass on a warning. But the story is arranged so that Trevor is nearby, earning a new boiler as a result of his prompt action.

Down the Drain

This story too is based on one of Bill Rogers' tales, and though I think it was not one within his personal experience, I have no reason to doubt its authenticity. Bad weather causes an area between the china clay quarry and the harbour at Brendam to flood, and Ben is stranded. Thomas comes to the rescue, and the Twins resolve never to tease him again. Maybe!

JOCK THE NEW ENGINE, (1990)

It had been my wish for some time to continue the Ravenglass & Eskdale-based saga Father had begun in *Small Railway Engines*. My father, after the earlier book, had developed an engine to 'match' the Ravenglass line's *Northern Rock* but had never had the chance to write stories about him – this became my opportunity. I was helped by the Sales Department at the publisher, for when my Editor pursed her lips dubiously at a book which did not mention Thomas, they said: "Great, a new engine – we've been hoping for one of them for years!"

We Need Another Engine

Frank is cross at being omitted from *Small Railway Engines* and collides with the Arlesburgh shed wall – he is later able to redeem himself by rescuing Rex after a steam-pipe failure. On the day of publication of *Small Railway Engines* (1967), *Perkins*, Frank's alter ego, really did collide with the shed wall, in annoyance, it was suggested, at not being in the new book. My family and I, in 1988, were on board a train that *Perkins* rescued after *River Esk's* steam-pipe failed. This story forms an example of two incidents, actually happening some while apart, coming together in a single story.

Sticking Power

A coupling breaks between Bert and his coaches at Arlesdale, but the broken parts are stuck together with glue and Bert is able to get his train home. Quickly, before loud howls of 'Impossible!" and "Don't be ridiculous!" arise, it is on record that an adhesive company once did precisely as described in the story as a publicity stunt for their product, on the Romney, Hythe & Dymchurch Railway.

Jock

The new engine, as yet without a name, appears in an odd shade of undercoat. Douglas, who happens to be nearby, says it reminds him of the old days when similarly-painted engines in Scotland (they would have belonged to the Highland Railway) were nicknamed 'Jocks'. Both the name and the colour stick.

Teamwork

Jock proves his worth with a container of sleepers, but his colleagues get a little weary of his boasting; finally between them, they prove the value of teamwork. The container incident is an authenticated Ravenglass story, but the rest of the tale, though I have a faint recollection of Father having told me something similar, is down to my fancy.

THOMAS AND THE GREAT RAILWAY SHOW, (1991)

The inspiration for this book was really a gentleman called Rob Shorland-Ball, who was on the staff of the National Railway Museum in the late 1980s when the roof of the Great Hall needed renewal and the concept of The Great Railway Show was born. He suggested that it would be nice if Thomas could be involved, and although it was a while before I worked out how it could be done in an authentic manner, this book was the result.

Museum-Piece

An introductory story really, though something like the level-crossing incident in which Thomas becomes involved did actually happen. Thomas is invited to York for The Great Railway Show and, amid a certain amount of rather jealous bickering from other engines, sets out on his journey. He is – literally – stopped in his tracks when he collides with a level-crossing gate.

Not the Ticket

Thomas arrives at York on a low-loader, but while the lorry-driver asks for directions to the NRM an officious traffic-warden slaps a parking ticket on the lorry. Some Christmases ago a locomotive belonging to the Nene Valley Railway was parked on a low-loader in Peterborough's old market square as part of a charity fund-raiser: the low-loader and its driver were given a parking ticket.

Trouble on the Line

This began as a cautionary tale, the idea of which was a warning to readers that steam locomotives can be dangerous and are unable to stop quickly. The story, in which Thomas becomes concerned about the crowds and then a lunch box falls in front of him, causes an emergency stop. This gradually became watered down between fears of fright to readers from the publishers and possible reflections on crowd-control arrangements from the

Museum, until it was but a shadow of its former self. A pity – the original version flowed far better as a story, and all we can do to show children that railways are not to be trifled with should, in my view, be encouraged. Thankfully, I was later invited by the British Transport Police to write a series of stories doing exactly that.

Thomas and the Railtour

Crowds are thronging to the steam-hauled railtours to the seaside (Scarborough, though it is not named in the story), and in order to cater for everyone strengthening the train – ie, adding extra carriages – becomes the only option, Thomas volunteers to help *Green Arrow* and, coupled in front on the way home, spots a landslip by the river near Kirkstead Abbey. Before going back to Sodor Thomas is given a plaque commemorating his visit.

THOMAS COMES HOME, (1992)

The title of this book is, I fear, a complete misnomer, but the publisher at the time insisted on dragging Thomas into it, despite the fact that Thomas appears only on the last page of the last story. The stories in fact tell of what happened on Thomas's branch line while he was away at York.

Snow Problem

Daisy, after bragging how much she likes snow, is stranded in a snowdrift near the airfield at Toryreck and finds she doesn't like it a bit: Harold comes to the rescue of the passengers and Daisy has to stay there for a week! Trains cut off in snow are no new thing, and for a week at a time is not unknown, but this one, with snow blocking Daisy's air-intake, has echoes of the 'wrong sort of snow' slip of the tongue which the Big Railway found so hard to live down.

Washout!

The bridge across the Hackenbeck Brook, just beyond the tunnel on Thomas's branch line, has been weakened by floodwater and collapses shortly after Percy, with Annie and Clarabel, crosses it. A similar story was told once in, I believe, *The Railway Magazine*, though I have unfortunately mislaid the precise reference.

Toby's Megatrain

This story is based on another Wisbech & Upwell incident, when an engine crew, with a very long train at the height of the fruit season, thought they could make it back to Wisbech but found that they couldn't. Like Toby when caught in a similar situation, they had to leave the train and go on to their destination to get water before returning to pick up the train. The crew's 'wheel-pull' on Toby is simply added whimsy.

Thomas Comes Home

Thomas is on his way back from York and the Fat Controller has arranged a 'welcome home' reception at Knapford Junction. But George the steamroller has been repairing the road at the level crossing between Knapford and Dryaw and, when the work is done, leaves behind a traffic cone which blows under Daisy, hurrying to the party. It damages her brakes, which need a fitter's attention but in spite of her misgivings she makes it in time – just. The cone/brake incident is authentic but the rest, other than the NRM plaque is pure fiction.

HENRY AND THE EXPRESS, (1993)

Out of Puff

Henry, with an excess of hot ash from poor coal collecting in his smokebox, suffers from a warped smokebox door and the consequent lack of a vacuum causes failure at Wellsworth. His driver and fireman use paper-mache to make an airtight seal inside his smokebox door, so that he can get his train home. Both the problem with the hot ash and the paper-mache seal are authentic, and I came across the latter when reading some years ago of a similar incident on the Somerset & Dorset Joint line.

Overhaul

Henry, on his way to the works for overhaul, is once again brought to a stand, this time near Killdane and this time as a driving-wheel tyre begins to disintegrate. He cannot get home on his own, and James, with whom he was double-heading, takes the train on. I quote *The Railway Magazine*, November 1924: "On Sunday October 5, 1924, a tyre became detached from one of the coupled wheels of the leading engine of double-headed Glasgow-London express while travelling at high speed near Weedon... The broken tyre caused considerable damage to the station, though luckily no-one was on the platform at the time."

Sliding Scales

James, during Henry's absence, is assigned to 'The Flying Kipper,' a job he hates: he is just about to leave the fish dock when a pile of fish-boxes falls from a forklift, across the rails in front of him. Scales and fish-oil make the rails slippery and its some time before

James finally finds his feet... This story is based on a 1950s incident when an LNER 2-6-0, following a fish train, found itself in trouble during a climb towards the Forth Bridge thanks to oil and scales that had leaked from one of the preceding fish vans.

Henry Sees Red

Henry's overhaul at Crovan's Gate is progressing, but he has not yet had a full repaint when an emergency needs him on the line. He comes to the rescue – but in a becoming pink undercoat. The particular incident on which this story is based is one involving a Stanier 'Jubilee' class locomotive in a similar situation, but I rather suspect that this isn't the only example of such a thing happening.

WILBERT THE FOREST ENGINE, (1994)

This book, I make no bones about it, was written in response to special pleading from the Dean Forest Railway, of which Father was then President. As with the earlier NRM book it was some time before I realised how I could, logically and authentically, transfer Wilbert to the Island of Sodor, but once that was solved the stories fell easily into place.

Percy's Porridge

In 1993 I was asked to visit Abingdon School in Middlesbrough to spend a morning with a class and work on a Thomas story with the children, As a starting point I posited an incident I had recently read about, where bags of maize in South Africa, had burst open on a railway during a heavy rainstorm. Though there were, as one might expect from children with no great experience of railways, a good many 'non railwaylike' suggestions for our story, I was able to go away afterwards and, with their permission, prepare a more 'authentic' version for publication.

Cab Over Wheels

I confess I cannot now recall chapter and verse for the incident which sparked off this story, but I have no doubt it is authenticated at wherever Austerity locomotive No.16 is now preserved. To cover for Percy's mishap, Wilbert is diverted to Thomas's branch line and in a tale which he tells in Ffarquhar shed to Thomas and Toby, No.16, much too big for his wheels, goes – literally – too far and topples down the side of a slag-bank in a steelworks.

Foaming at the Funnel

This story is based on one my Uncle George told me of an engine which was inadvertently taken to a milk-loading stand instead of to the water tower. Need one say more? The dairy in question here is at Elsbridge. But a title – almost always the last thing I do with a story – eluded me for some time until I suddenly realised that a phrase I had written in the middle of it would do admirably.

Wired-up

Wilbert, having done his emergency duty on Thomas's branch line, now moves to where he had originally been intended for, the branch between Tidmouth and Arlesburgh. The causality for the book envisages that the Fat Controller wishes to assess the capabilities of a 0-6-0 Austerity tank engine with a view to obtaining one to help the branch. During a visit to Arlesburgh, Wilbert meets the small railway engines and is able to suggest a way that a problem with a broken coupling might be overcome. I can find no note of this incident in any of my records: I suspect I must have read it – perhaps in *Steam Railway* or somewhere similar – and used it almost at once without recording it.

THOMAS AND THE FAT CONTROLLER'S ENGINES, (1995)

This book was planned as *The Fat Controller's Engines*, which makes more sense in the context of the stories, until a last-minute publisher's unilateral decision altered it – it wouldn't have been so galling had they not asked me to the annual Sales Conference to talk about it beforehand. I can only imagine that the change was made at the request of the sales force. The book was written, anyway, to celebrate in 1995 the 50th anniversary of the publication of the first book in the Railway Series in May 1945.

Birdstrike

Gordon, in full cry with the express, raises a cloud of crows in front of him, one of which collides with the vacuum brake pipe and knocks out the stopper. As mentioned in the story, an incident like this happened on the Great Western in 1915.

Edward and the Cabbages

Edward, hurrying one day, loses a bogie wheel, which bounds along beside the train until it disappears into a field of cabbages. This story, not it has to be admitted, very different in idea from the earlier one about Henry – see Overhaul, above, is based on a separate unidentified and undated cutting in my father's scrapbook.

Rabbits

Near the airfield station on Thomas's branch line is a short, steep hill – rabbits have undermined this, but before anything can be done about it the track goes wide of gauge and Thomas is derailed. Rolvenden bank, on the Kent & East Sussex Railway, also undermined by rabbits and repaired at great expense, was the starting point for this story, and the method of re-railing Thomas described has been confirmed by permanent way staff as what they might do in similar circumstances.

Golden Jubilee

A 'could have happened' story this one, for a funnel spider, weaving a web among the electrics of a signalbox could, I am assured by personnel at the National Environmental Research Council cause exactly this sort of disruption. The story is, otherwise an excuse to collect all the engines together for a 50th-anniversary celebration.

NEW LITTLE ENGINE, (1996)

Speedkiller

Problems with slipping after the weedkilling train has passed by have been experienced on the Ravenglass & Eskdale Railway, so why not on the Skarloey Railway too? Rheneas is brought to a stand but bravely manages to get his train to the end of the line.

Sir Handel's Plan

The Talyllyn Railway's engines are far too well-behaved for anything like this to have happened there, but their No.3 does use firebars which have to be specially ordered. Feeling disgruntled, Sir Handel decides that his firebars collapse is a good opportunity for a rest. But the staff are working on a new engine and no-one has time to spare for Sir Handel...

Dirty Water

Peter Sam tells a story of an incident while he was on the Talyllyn Railway when a problem with the water softening procedure caused him to 'prime' and make him emit sludgy water from his funnel. He is reminded of this episode by two visitors from the Talyllyn, Lizi and Kathy (see People, above), and retells the story at their prompting. He tells how he was put on to the centre road (ie spare track) so that visitors could see him and would not be disappointed at missing him, but, one gathers, it was not a day he much enjoyed.

I Name This Engine

Mr Ivo Hugh (see People, above) is to perform the naming of the new engine, but only the Thin Controller knows what the name is to be, and he's not saying. There are various adventures on the way to the event, and we finally discover why everyone, including Ivo Hugh, has been kept in the dark. In 1990 the Talyllyn launched *Tom Rolt*, the *alter ego* of Ivo Hugh, which was named by Tom Rolt's widow. Though Father never had time to write the story, he worked out a name for his new engine that fitted exactly, even down to the number of letters in each of the two names – perhaps intended as a final tribute to a man whom he had regarded highly.

THOMAS AND VICTORIA, (2007)

Overloaded

A simple story based on an incident on the Wisbech-Upwell Tramway, when fully laden carriages carried passengers on the end Verandahs. A near accident resulted in a ban at the practice for safety reasons. Henrietta's overloading became so frequent that arrangements needed to be made for extra accommodation.

Avalanche

The 'extra accommodation' is a coach from Edward's old railway and while she is being repaired, she tells of an incident that happened in the 'old' days.

Eels on Wheels

Daisy often sees grass snakes basking beside the line in hot weather but gets very upset when a box of similar creatures falls on the line in front of her.

Toby's Vintage Train

Victoria, the old coach, is now repaired and Edward takes her to Thomas' Junction. An incident with Terence causes a problem but Thomas and Victoria finally get through to join Toby's vintage train.

THOMAS AND HIS FRIENDS, (2011)

This book was published as a tribute in the centenary year of the Rev. W Awdry's birth.

Thomas and the Swan

A swan injures itself by flying into the parapet of the bridge, over the river at Elsbridge. Thomas and his crew rescue the bird and take it to the Vet where it recovers safely. Something of this sort must have happened frequently at railways over the years.

Buffer Bashing

Donald has an unfortunate incident on a frosty day with a set of buffers. Later, Douglas, after scoffing at such clumsy behaviour, has a similar incident involving red paint. Though I have now unfortunately lost my record of the original incident, I know this did occur on an engine's unfortunate collision with a pair of freshly painted red buffers.

Gordon's Fire Service

One day Gordon is stopped near his viaduct by a man waving his arms. A straw bale is on fire but thankfully Gordon is on hand to save the day.

Centenary

This is the story of how The Fat Controller's Railway celebrated the centenary of my father's birth.

Thomas: A Crown Worth Fighting For

This year, as anyone with the stamina to have read this far will be aware, sees the 80th anniversary of the publication of the first volume in my father's 'Railway Series' and this volume will, if all goes to plan, be available in time to mark its own 20th anniversary of the first edition. It was originally planned (2005) partly because it seemed at one stage that neither Hit Entertainment, owners of the Thomas 'Rights' (at that time) nor the company it franchises to produce the books (Egmont Publishing Ltd) seemed likely to do anything to celebrate the impending Diamond Jubilee, but largely because so many people were writing and asking about Father's earlier book, *The Island of Sodor, its People, History and Railways*. This book, published by Kaye & Ward in 1987, had been out of print for almost 15 years. One of the things omitted from that book was any detail about the stories themselves. This omission the present volume has set out to correct and has brought the information about the whole Series up to date.

As of 2011 there has not been a new title in the Series. The fact that the entire Series was to be re-formatted was given as an excuse not to do a new book for 1997, but after re-vamping a mere 14 this plan collapsed when the public made it clear that the revised format was disliked, and nothing new (in regard to the Railway Series) has appeared since 2011. Ever since, and particularly since 2002, I have been repeatedly asked when something new is coming, to which my somewhat lame reply has, of necessity, been something like:- "I suggest you ask the publishers, because they are not asking me."

In January 2005, a meeting was arranged with one of the Directors of Egmont Publishing, and we explained that it was becoming deeply embarrassing while acting as, in effect, their unpaid agents at Thomas events up and down the country, to have to say to people to who wanted a signature in one of my own books that a mere handful was available. The gentleman seemed unaware of a very large body of material – some 40 titles – lying out of print, but to his credit he did ask to see photographs of the covers in case anything could be done. He also said he would be pleased to see any new material that I cared to submit. While this is a long way from saying that new stories will be available soon, I at least had not been idle and had on hand two new Railway Series books and seven other 'Thomas' stories, which were published in 2007 and 2011. But since then, nothing.

The survival of Thomas, as with the earlier Beatrix Potter series, depends upon the original stories. All the other stuff is ephemeral and titles produced for a cheap and quick turnover in 2002 are already forgotten. Fortunately a rethink quickly re-introduced the original format so all was not lost.

The man at Egmont referred to boxed sets of both Father's and my contributions to the series, which is a step forward, certainly, but not the answer for the child or parent who has, in the first instance perhaps only a fiver to spend and in the second 30 of the 42 books already and may be faced with a bill of £200 or more for two boxes in order to complete his/her set. Who can blame them for fixing on something different? As to the outcome of this saga only time will tell – my contributions are now all out of print anyway and Father's set is to mark the 80th anniversary of the publication of his first book.

So perhaps the future can only get better. Someone remarked the other day that if my father could see he wouldn't just be spinning in his grave but humming as well! It is also true, happily, that the children who visit Thomas events up and down the country generally have a whale of a time, as did we back when we visited. Back in the day, between February and October 2005, 115 or more weekends were taken up with a Day Out With Thomas event on some railway or another in the UK and, sadly, there was no possibility that we could get to all of them – our tally was a mere eight, in among various other events in the Thomas interest and tours of Canada and Scotland – but we certainly enjoyed them. Sadly nowadays, due to the expense there are far fewer Days Out With Thomas. But if you are lucky enough to go to one, we hope you will enjoy it and maybe acquire what we once heard described as "...our first item of Thomas regalia."

Thomas, we feel, **still has** a crown and it is worth fighting for.

And Finally... Behind the Curtain

The idea to re-publish this book started a couple of years ago, whilst myself and my wife Helen were getting ready to move home and being forced (downsizing I believe is the correct terminology) to empty our garage of all the boxes that had accumulated over the years. As well as spiders, old lamps, dust covered railway magazines and rusty tools that I shall never use again, I found a number of boxes. And once I peeked inside I began to smile. For I remembered seeing them years before, thinking that perhaps Father had given them away to a museum or such. But then I remembered, he had left them to me. And that's where they had sat, never seen before in the public domain, forgotten that is, until today.

Then, most recently, I was told of the abhorrent prices that Sodor Reading Between the Lines was being sold for online, prompting me to take action. Its one thing for fans to pay fair price for your works, but quite another to see people being taken advantage of to the tune of £300-400. So, I decided to do something about it. I contacted someone I knew in the industry, asked them if they'd be interested in preparing the book for re-publication, and that is what you now have in your hands. Hopefully I might add, at a far more reasonable price, something that was always important to Father to, ensuring the works were accessible by all.

'But', my newly acquired publisher had said, 'wouldn't it be better to make the second edition different? Perhaps add something that the fans wouldn't have seen before?' And that is how I decided on the use of Father's original documentation, found in my garage and how we now have this '20th Anniversary' revised edition.

We authors are solitarily creatures, we work alone, rarely, if ever, telling you the reader what is going on inside our heads. You only get to see the finished product, the glossy hardback book, or the shiny new paperback. Months or perhaps even years of planning go into the book, with edits, omissions and endless re-writes. The story is written and taken as gospel, rumours can be started by fans whilst forums on the internet can buzz with the 'what if's' or the 'whys'. Authors sit back happily content to allow the speculation and rumours run wild, after all, if people are talking about your books, then all the better. But what if you could peek behind the curtain? What if you could see written in their own hand the thoughts and ideas that led them to make a decision or their meticulous attention to detail in getting the book over the finish line. That Ladies and Gentleman, boys and girls is what I am about to reveal to you today. I cannot of course guarantee that the following will answer all of the thousands of questions that are out there, but for some, perhaps, this little glimpse may prove helpful, interesting and enjoyable.

Please note, these documents are old and originally the publisher wanted to 'digitally' tidy them up. I have declined to to do this as I believe their age adds to their charm and authenticity. Where I believe necessary I shall transcribe the letters. Regards the maps, those viewing with a digital device I am reliably informed will be able to simply zoom in, and to those readers using a more 'traditional' approach we have printed the illustrations on their sides to make viewing them all the more easier.

So lets sit back together and look at some of my father's work as we take a peek around the curtain...

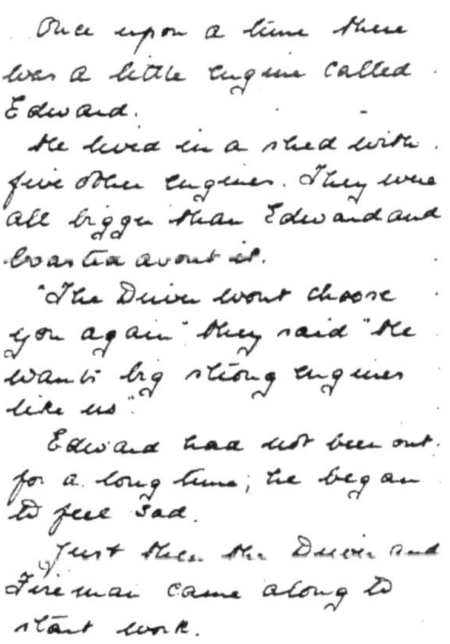

Once upon a time there was a little engine called Edward.
He lived in a shed with five other engines. They were all bigger than Edward and boasted about it.
"The Driver won't choose you again" they said "He wants big strong engines like us".
Edward had not been out for a long time; he began to feel sad.
Just then the Driver and Fireman came along to start work.

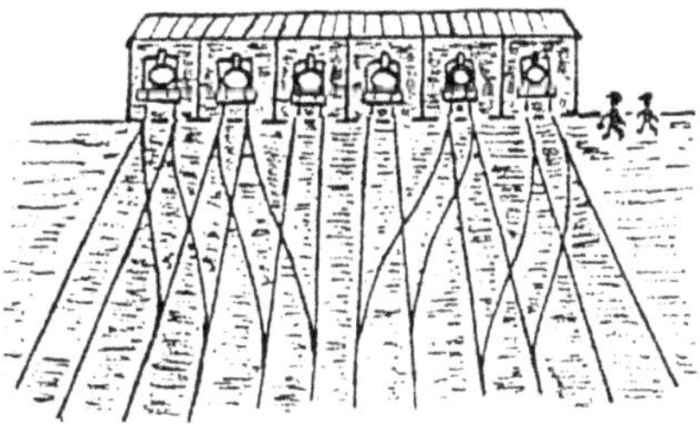

Above - Where it all began 80 years ago, Father's notes and the rough sketch for the first book in The Railway Series.

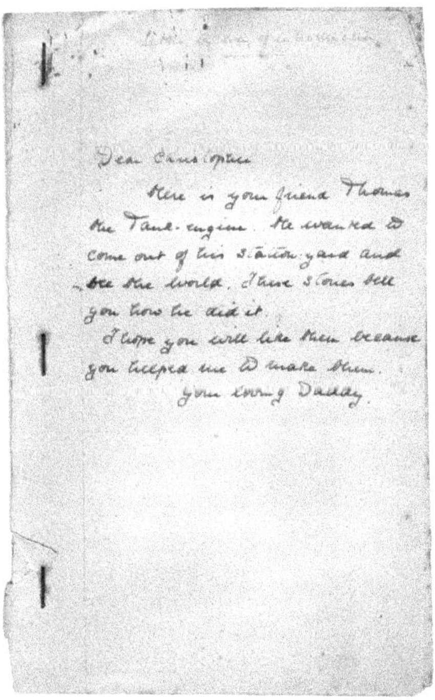

Dear Christopher
Here is your friend Thomas the Tank-engine. He wanted to come out of his station-yard and see the world. These stories tell you how he did it.
I hope you will like them because you helped me to make them.
Your loving Daddy.

Left - The first official Thomas book hand written by my father.

'Dear Christopher here is your friend Thomas the Tank-engine. He wanted to come out of his station-yard and see the world. These stories tell you how he did it. I hope you will like them because you helped me to make them. Your loving Daddy.'

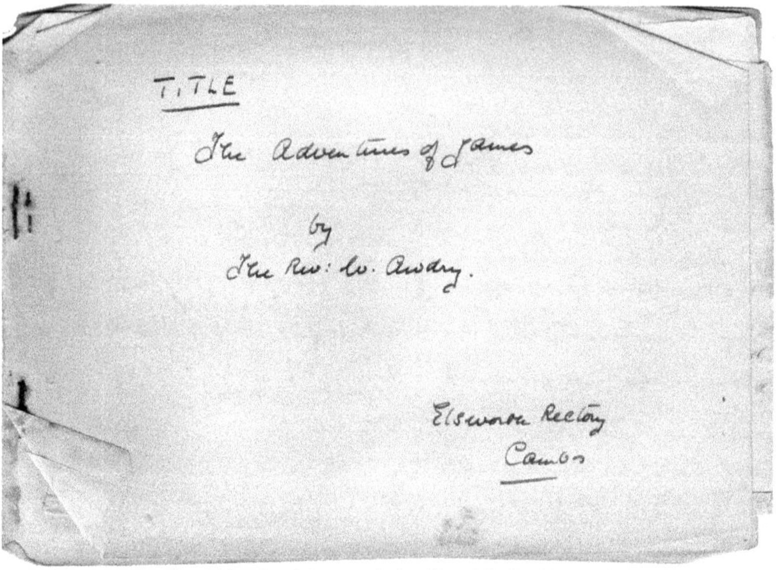

Above - 'James the Red Engine' was originally titled 'The Adventures of James'

Below - Correspondence from E Ward showing the original illustrator's lack of railway engineering knowledge.

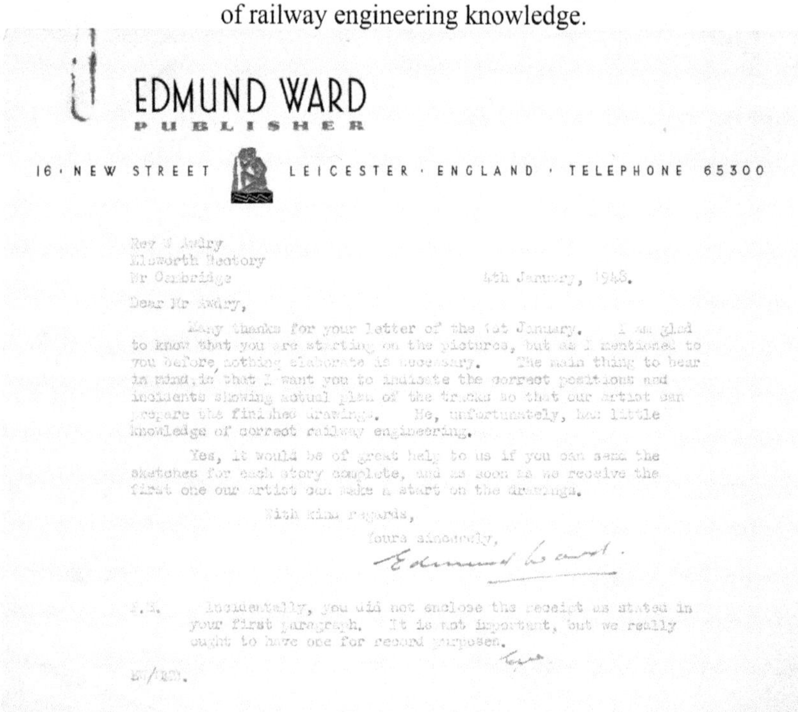

EDMUND WARD
PUBLISHER

16 · NEW STREET LEICESTER · ENGLAND · TELEPHONE 65300

Rev W Awdry
Elsworth Rectory
Nr Cambridge

4th January, 1948.

Dear Mr Awdry,

Many thanks for your letter of the 1st January. I am glad to know that you are starting on the pictures, but as I mentioned to you before, nothing elaborate is necessary. The main thing to bear in mind, is that I want you to indicate the correct positions and incidents showing actual plan of the tracks so that our artist can prepare the finished drawings. He, unfortunately, has little knowledge of correct railway engineering.

Yes, it would be of great help to us if you can send the sketches for each story complete, and as soon as we receive the first one our artist can make a start on the drawings.

With kind regards,

Yours sincerely,

P.S. Incidentally, you did not enclose the receipt as stated in your first paragraph. It is not important, but we really ought to have one for record purposes.

EW/[illegible].

Below - Correspondence from Father's publisher who was already hinting at a change of title and to incorperate British Railways, which was formed earlier that same year.

EDMUND WARD

PUBLISHER

16 · NEW STREET LEICESTER · ENGLAND · TELEPHONE 65300

The Rev W Awdry
Elsworth Rectory
Cambridge

3rd March 1948

Dear Mr Awdry,

I have greatly enjoyed reading through the four new stories "The Adventures of James". These will make a nice little companion book for the other two, but I think perhaps we ought to make a few slight alterations.

As it will be some months before we can publish the book, we ought to mention "British Railways", which will then be an accepted fact, even by small boys.

I think it would be better to have some sort of railway flavour in the title, and I would suggest JAMES JOINS BRITISH RAILWAYS. The Fat Director could then become the Fat Controller. Don't you think it would make the story more topical? I rather like the name of "Jeremiah Jobling" for the man with the bowler. The change to British Railways could be described by a short foreword to take the place of the note to Christopher in "Thomas the Tank Engine". Will you let me know what you think about this? and, if you agree, perhaps you will let me have the wording for the foreword.

I shall be pleased to see your suggestions for the sketches and I will arrange to let you examine the finished drawings before we put the plates in hand. This time, I want to make the book really good.

With kind regards,

Yours sincerely,

Edmund Ward.

P.S. I shall be pleased to send you cheque for half the amount now if you wish & balance when your sketches are complete. E.W.

Below - All part of the process. Correspondence from Father to the then editor at E Ward, Mr Marriot with the 'roughs' for *Thomas and the Guard*. For the benefit of those that struggle to read my father's writing I will translate below...

ETLM/CMB.

Elsworth Rectory
Cambs
Jan 20th 1949

Dear Mr Marriott

Here are the 'roughs' for this week
The Story is "Thomas and the Guard"

(1) General view of Thomas, Annie & Clarabel from front. Any sort of country for background and foreground will do

(2) View of Annie and Clarabel from behind. I have tried with the aid of windows and a queer handle thing sometimes seen on Coaches to give Clarabel an expression of cheerful Complacency, but have only succeeded in making her look somewhat malevolent.

(3) Thomas and Henry at the junction. Thomas I think should look crosser than I have made him, and the platform between them should be <u>wider</u> than I have shown.

(4) has completely stumped me.
It is intended to illustrate (on page 4)
"The guard turned round to jump into his
van, tripped over an old lady's umbrella, and
fell flat on his face. By the time he picked
himself up, Thomas, and Annie and Clarabel
were steaming out of the Station.
The train, platform etc were alright, but
the Shelter over the platform (cf page
13 James the Red Engine) as seen from
underneath has completely defeated me.
The left hand side has worked in alright
but I cannot manage the right hand side.
There should be a lot of people and luggage
on the platform, but I leave that to your
artist, he can draw people and I can't

Yours Sincerely

W Awdry

'Dear Mr Marriot
Here are the 'roughs' for this week. The story is Thomas and the Guard

1. *General view of Thomas, Annie and Clarabel from front. Any sort of Country for background and foreground will do.*

2. *Views of Annie and Clarabel from behind. I have tried with the aid of windows and a queer handle thing sometimes seen on coaches to give Clarabel an expression of Cheerful complacency, but have only succeeded in making the look somewhat malevolent.*

3. *Thomas and Henry at the junction. Thomas I think should look crosser than I have made him, and the platform between them should be wider than I have shown.*

4. *Has completely stumped me. It is intended to illustrate (on page 4) 'The guard turned round to jump into his van, tripped over an old lady's umbrella, and fell flat on his face. By the time he picked himself up, Thomas and Annie and Clarabel were steaming out of the station. The train, platform etc were alright but the shelter over the platform (eg page 13 James the Red Engine) as seen from underneath has completely defeated me. The left hand side has worked in alright but I can't manage the right hand side. There should be a lot of people and luggage on the platform, and I leave that to your artist, he can draw people and I can't. Yours Sincerely W V Awdry.'*

Here we see a perfect example of Father's resourcefulness.
On one torn side (above) we have a detailed map of Knapford Junction, drawn for the benefit of the illustrator Dalby. Whilst (below) we have the Elsworth Carol Service for New Years Day 1950. Father would grab whatever was to hand if he had an idea that he wanted writing down, be it newspapers or hymn sheets.

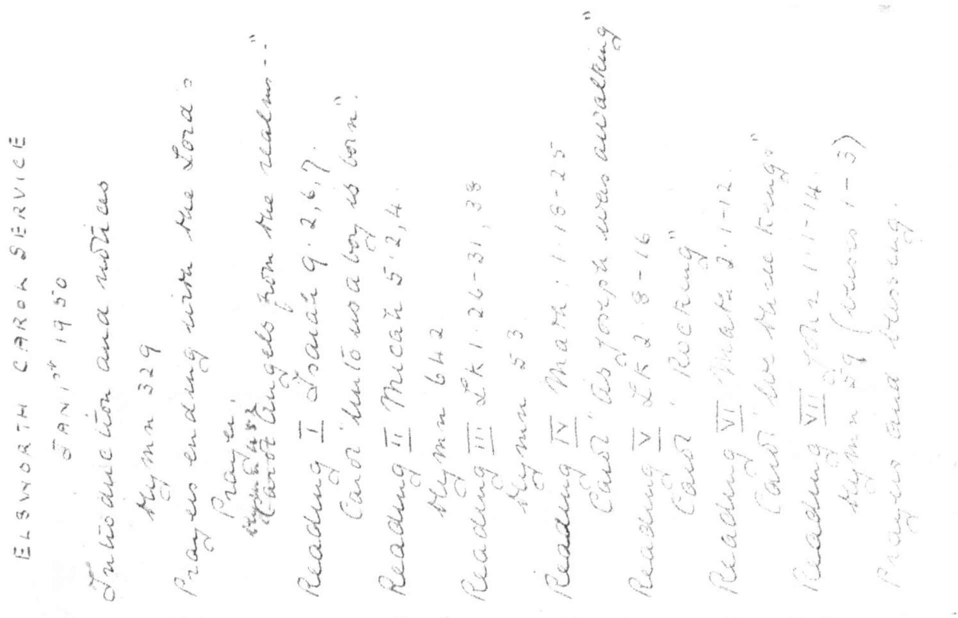
ELSWORTH CAROL SERVICE
JAN 1st 1950
Introduction and notices
Hymn 329
Prayers ending with the Lord's Prayer
Carol 'Angels from the realms'
Reading I Isaiah 9. 2,6,7.
Carol 'Unto us a boy is born'
Reading II Micah 5. 2,4
Hymn 642
Reading III Lk 1. 26-31, 38
Hymn 53
Reading IV Matt. 1. 18-25
Carol 'As Joseph was awalking'
Reading V Lk 2. 8-16
Carol 'Rocking'
Reading VI Matt. 2. 1-12
Carol 'We three Kings'
Reading VII John 1. 1-14
Hymn 59 (verses 1-5)
Prayers and blessing.

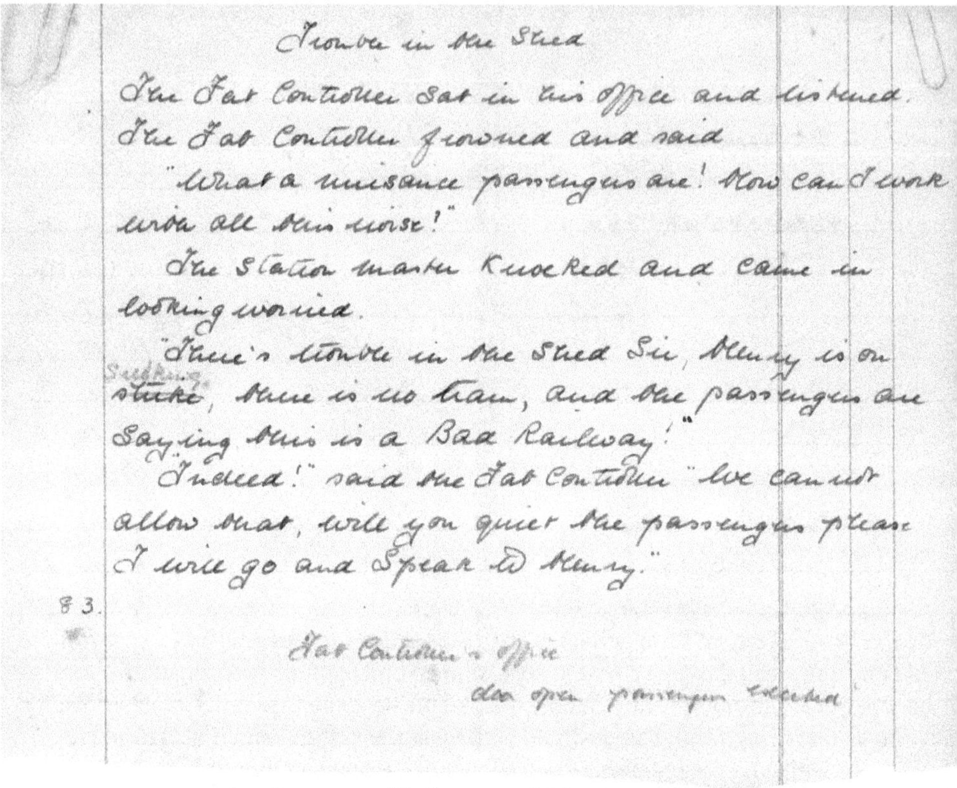

Trouble in the Shed

The Fat Controller sat in his office and listened.
The Fat Controller frowned and said
"What a nuisance passengers are! How can I work with all this noise!"
The Station master knocked and came in looking worried.
"There's trouble in the Shed Sir, Henry is on Sulking strike, there is no train, and the passengers are saying this is a Bad Railway!"
"Indeed!" said the Fat Controller "We cannot allow that, will you quiet the passengers please I will go and speak to Henry."

83.

Fat Controller's office
door open passengers collected

Another case of Father not wishing to waste paper.
Above the draft for 'Trouble in the Shed' but turn over the same paper and we have something I can only describe as 'accounting' from 1926!
Point to note, you can see from above that when Father was creating the draft he would describe briefly the illustration (Fat Controller's office, door open passengers collected) before later going into detail with the illustrator.

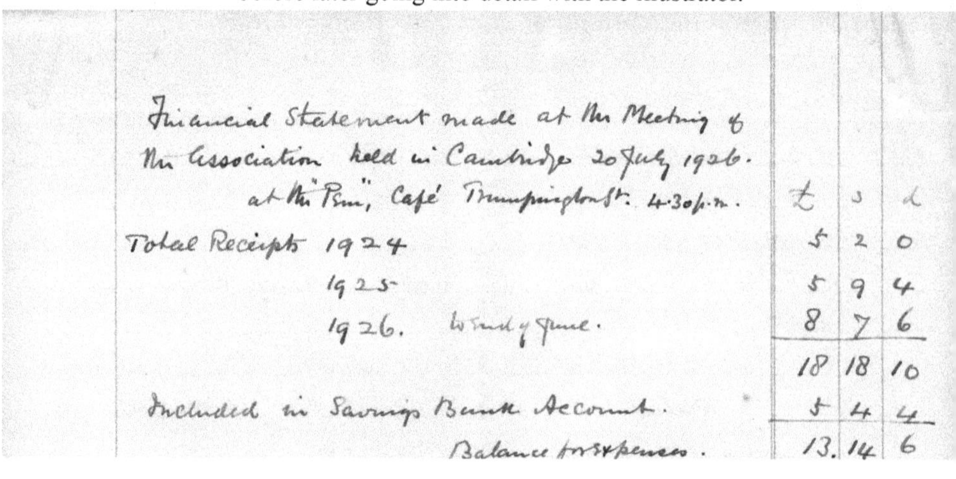

Financial Statement made at the Meeting of the Association held in Cambridge 20 July 1926. at the "Bun" Café Trumpington St. 4·30 p.m.

	£	s	d
Total Receipts 1924	5	2	0
1925	5	9	4
1926. to end of June.	8	7	6
	18	18	10
Included in Savings Bank Account.	5	4	4
Balance for expenses.	13.	14	6

Percy and the Trousers.
Above a rough sketch showing what Father envisaged, whilst below we see his notes for Dalby.
(translated on the next page)

Percy & the Trousers

I

Percy and Henry (in tunnel shape) somewhere in the yard
I would suggest a sea background
- a posh morning - workmen about with mufflers on.
Henry should have an offended expression. Percy has just been rude about his funnel.

II - There is merely an indication porter (left) is manoeuvering a heavily loaded trolley down the ramp.
Percy is sneaking in behind
On second thought it would be better to have porter coming from the other platform.
This would avoid overloading left hand of picture & leaving right hand bare.
Station details to be added of course passengers porters luggage other things
Percy is on the extreme right hand of the three tracks - which is the arrival line
- last coach of train not visible
- it is drawn up at the right hand platform

(3) Percy halted after the crash
The text gives details as to his appearance
Smashed luggage
Angry passengers & Controller etc.
Station details

'Percy and the Trousers.

1 Percy and Henry (in his new shape) somewhere in the yard. I would suggest a sea background – a frosty morning – workers about with mufflers on. Henry should have an offended expression, Percy has just been rude about his funnel.

2 This is merely an indication porter (left) is manoeuvring a heavily loaded trolley down the ramp. Percy is sneaking in behind. On second thoughts though it would be better to have porter coming from the office platform. This would avoid overloading left hand of picture and leaving right hand bare. Station details to be added of course, passengers, porters, luggage – other things. Percy is on the extreme right hand of the three tracks which is of course the arrival line -Last coach of train not visible – it is drawn up at the right hand platform.

3 Percy halted after crash. The desc (description) gives details as his appearance, Smashed luggage, angry passengers, F. Controller etc. Station details...'

Over the next few pages you can see some more examples of my father's request to Dalby for illustrations of *The Flying Kipper* in which he goes into great detail describing what the interior of the guards van should look like.

Dear Mr Dalby Feb 9th 1951

Here are some suggestions to help with picture V "The Flying Kipper"

P.G. (a) outside of brake van – not really relevant for the picture, but might be useful for any points not included in (b) & (c)

N B the picture does not show (unfortunately) a van with look out windows see (c) but general shape is correct for my purpose

(b) gives side view of brake ~~handle~~ ~~top~~ handle & standard (top view given in (c)) height about 3ft 3 length of handle X 2ft 6.

(C) plan of inside of van.

details not shown

1. The oil lamp hung from roof
2. oil lamp on bracket to light desk
3. three spare tail lamps (two white & one red) hung on the ~~[illegible]~~ hooks by stove
4. Guards lamp on bracket on seat where indicated – red & green flags rolled up would be closely either on the seat or hung handy from a bracket on the wall

My idea of picture would be three men round the

stove – Guard, on left looking at watch – sitting on padded seat with back to look out window

– Driver standing centre

– Fireman sitting on plain seat (right) close to Guard's lamp bracket with mug of cocoa.

– Moving light through window – but not light enough in van to do without lighted lamps.

I hope these ideas are helpful. With all good wishes

Yours sincerely

W. V. Awdry

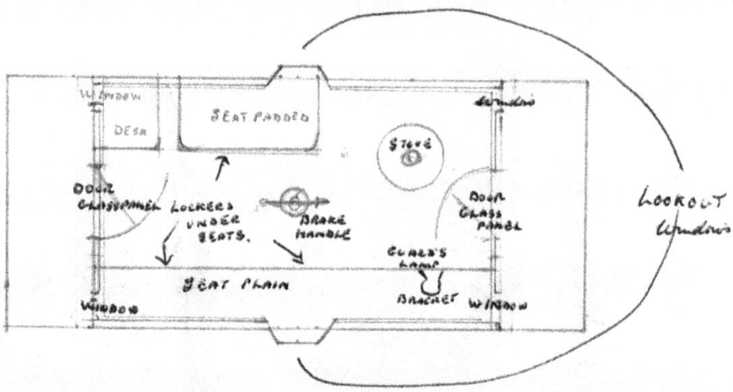

By this stage Father knew the extent of Dalby's lack of railway engineering knowledge and sought to help where he could, as you can see by his description of what the signal should look like. Interestingly Father at this stage had not put numbers on the engines. Something which he now asks for. You can see the publisher's reply.

IV

view from Drivers side of Cab. In my previous notes I said this should be the left side - this however varies and the most general I find is the right side as shown in this photograph.

picture can be used as it is - clean out locomotive name plate of course and insert distant signal in the roughly where I have put it

- warning light - objects discernible - distant signal at danger. this sketch not to Scale shows general shape & colouring

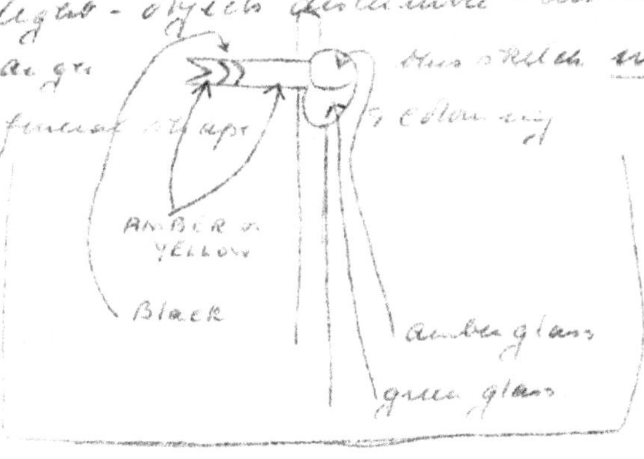

Snow etc all around - indicate that fall of snow there has been fairly heavy.

I hope this will help

One more thing would you please put numbers on the engines in addition to Thomas - yellow or gold with red outside lines similar to Thomas

The correct numbers are

THOMAS	1
EDWARD	2
Henry	3
Gordon	4
James	5
Percy	6

Position of numbers

Edward, Henry, Gordon, James

numbers same size as Thomas'

but drawn on side of tender

in centre.

Percy's number goes on his

bunker not as with

Thomas on the

straight tanks

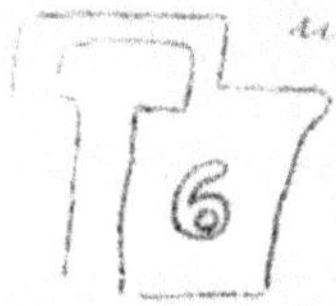

With all good wishes.

Yours sincerely

W V Awdry

EDMUND WARD

PUBLISHER

16 · NEW STREET LEICESTER · ENGLAND · TELEPHONE 65300

Rev W Awdry
Elsworth Rectory
Cambridge

13th February, 1951.

Dear Mr Awdry,

I am very sorry not to have acknowledged the receipt of your latest suggestions before now, but unfortunately sickness in the office has rather inconvenienced us.

I note that you now wish for numbers to be put on all the Engines. We should have done this from the start of course, but I am afraid that we shall be unable to make the necessary corrections at present in the first five books. However, in order to explain this innovation, will you please add something to the foreword of HENRY THE GREEN ENGINE in explanation? There is, of course, no reason why the Engines should not have been repainted and numbers added accordingly.

Yours sincerely,
for EDMUND WARD

E.T.L.Marriott Editor.
ETLM/MEC

Here we see the creation of 'Henrietta' for *Toby the Tram Engine*. As you can see my father mentions this is to be "...a little different to the usual."

Toby the Tram Engine

28/11/51

Dear Mr Dalby.

Here is a picture of Henrietta for you to use. She is the four wheeled coach and will give you something a little different from the usual.

Two unusual features (a) the verandah each end with the iron work railings

(b) Henrietta as can be seen from the photograph (Railway Magazine Dec 1950 Page 826) is about two foot lower in height than usual. Lower in fact, than Toby. The wheels are 2ft 3 in diameter as compared with 3ft 6 which is the usual size for coach wheels and the axleboxes and springs are smaller too.

(c) The coach is lighted by gas - note the curious shaped ventilators which are placed along the CENTRE LINE of the roof.

<u>Colour</u> - she is for the first three stories very dirty.

- Many years ago she was painted the VARNISHED TEAK COLOUR of the London & North Eastern Railway and traces of that colour still remain, though the paint has begun to flake off in places.
- Traces of a five figure number beginning 60 are visible, but not decipherable.

I hope these details will help.

Yours sincerely, W V Awdry

'Dear Mr Dalby

Here is a picture of Henrietta for you to use. She is a four wheeled coach and will give you something a little different from the usual.

Two unusual features (a) The verandah each end with the iron work railings (b) Henrietta as you can see from the photograph (Railway Magazine Dec 1950 page 826) is about two foot down in height than usual. Lower in fact than Toby. All wheels are 2ft 3 in diameter as compared with 3ft 6in which is the usual size in coach wheels and the axleboxes and springs are smaller too.

The coach is lighted by gas – note the curious shaped ventilation which are placed along the CENTRELINE of the roof.

Colour – she is for the first three stories very dirty.

-many years ago she was painted the VARNISHED TEAK colour of the London & North Eastern Railway and traces of that colour still remain, though the paint has begun to flake off in places.

-Traces of a five figure number beginning 60... are visible, but not decipherable.

I hope these details will help.

Yours Sincerely, W V Awdry'

By 1953 Father had realised that simply grabbing random pieces of paper to write his latest ideas upon was just simply not going do, and decided, thankfully, to use notebooks (or so I thought), and it was one of these such items re-discovered in our garage that I turn to now. The notebook in question contained notes and sketches for the stories of *Toby the Tram Engine.*

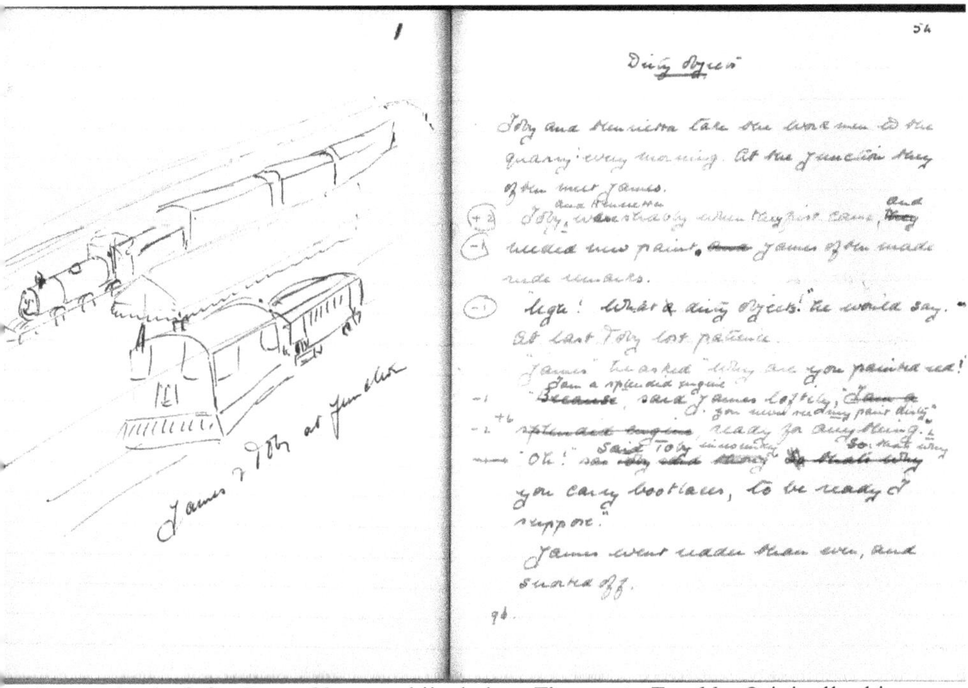

Above - the draft for *Dirty Objects* whilst below *Thomas in Trouble.* Originally this was to be called *Thomas and the Police* and featured a slightly different story.

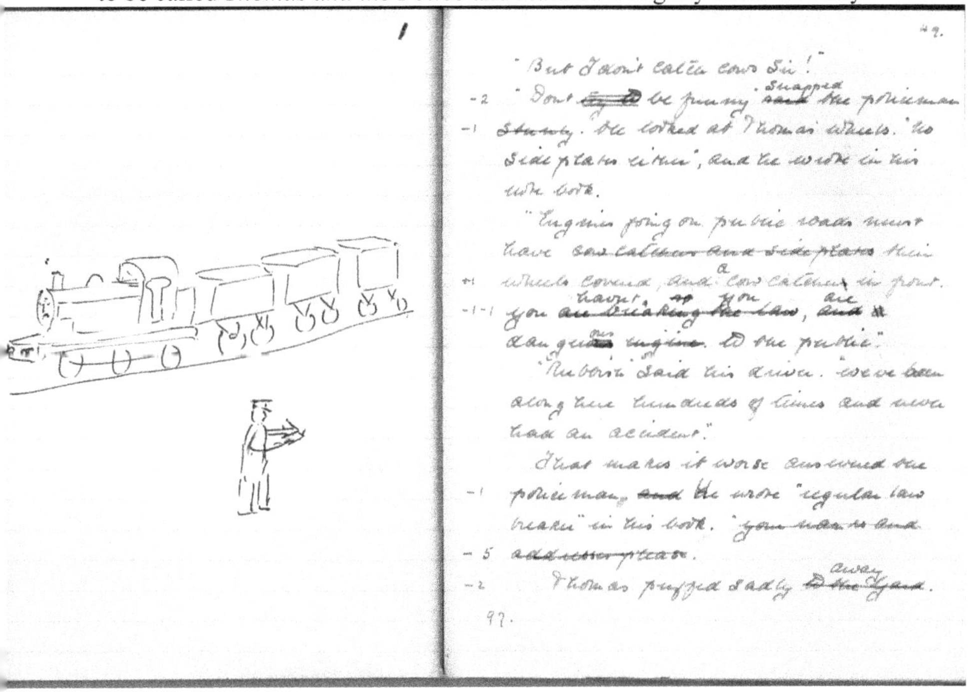

Here we see Father's 'roughs' for *Down the Mine* over the following pages. But, remember what I said about Father now using notebooks? As you can see over the next page all is not what it seems...

DOWN THE MINE

Picture II The Intermediate
Scene at the junction.
Gordon facing ~~west~~ north - travelling to Tidmouth - on left hand road of main station
Thomas also facing ~~west~~ north but pushing coaches - smoke shows direction of travel.

LAY OUT OF Station

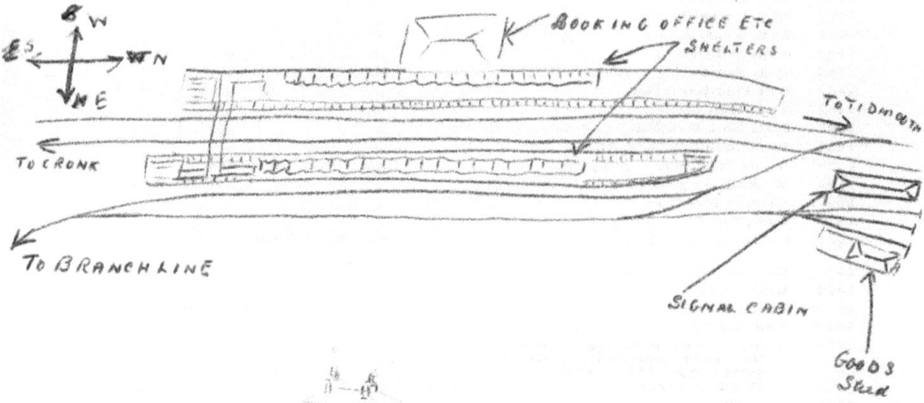

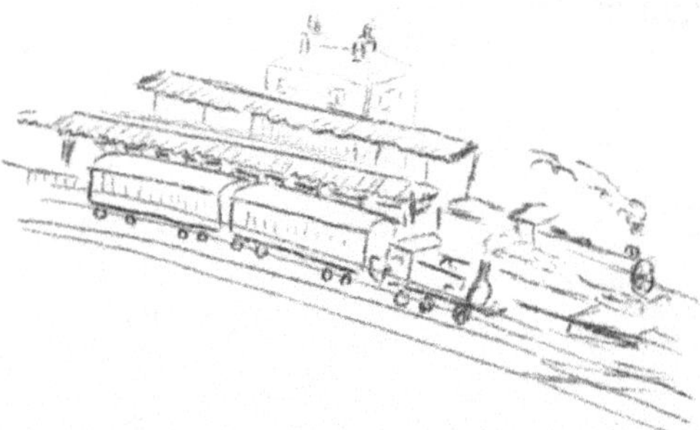

Rough Sketch
Suggesting picture
This is a different
view of junction to
any that we have
had before.

On one side a childrens story, on the other a list of Rectors of the Church of All Saints. A historical reminder that my father was both an author, and member of the Clergy. If you look closely you can see this information (despite our best efforts) shows through on the following pages as Father clearly had a number of pages of this list!

Rectors of the Church of All Saints, Staughton Parva.

Compiled from the Episcopal Registers of Lincoln, and from other Public Records.

1245	Henry de Etton ?		Patron—The Master of the Templars in England.
12..	Mag. Luke de Stratton†		,, ,,
1263	Dom. Philip†		,, ,,
1232	William de la River§		,, ,,
12..	Wm. de Strode† §		,, ,,
1300	Ric. de la More		,, ,,
1301	Wm. de Mundham		,, ,,
1330	John de Borham		,, Knights of St. John.
1379	Mag. John Ludeseye		,, ,,
1383	Dom. Wm. Osgodby	Patron, Ric. Gregory, jun.	,, ,,
1387	Dom. Henry Bokelond	,, Ric. Gregory, of Bekenesfeld	,, ,,
1388	Ric. Eland	,, John Pope, of Melcheburn	,, ,,
1389	Dom. Wm. Wylughton	,, ,, ,,	,, ,,
1390	John Hanerbergh		,, ,,
1398	Wm. de Pychthorn		,, ,,
13..	Mag. S. Halles	resigned	,, ,,
1408	Mag. Walter Trengof		,, ,,
1419	Dom. Thos. Broke		,, ,,
1443	Edward Lytell†		,, ,,
1445	John Benet	resigned	,, ,,
1453	Rob. Passelewe, B.A.	,,	,, ,,
1462	Dom. Wm. Corker		,, ,,
1507	Dom. Rob. Wadyluf†	Pension of vjs, viijd	,, ,,
1531	Dom. John Smyth, B.A.†		,, ,,
1554	Robert Wakerley	resigned	Patron—Oliver Leder, Esq.
1556	Sir Anth. Hopkin		,, Sir Oliver Leeder, Knt. 1554.
1559	Thomas Wilsonne		
1572	Thos. Noxe		
1573	Robert Condall, B.D.		Patron—Mr. Baldwin.
16..	Michael Hewes†	Buried Oct. 9th, 1612‡	
1612	Henry Gale†	,, Aug. 16th, 1639.	
1639	Henry Gering		Patron—Corpus Christi College, Oxon.¶
1644	Noel Sparke		,, ,,
1644	William Lake, B.D., sequestered 19th Dec., 1644, reinstated July 5th, 1647, buried Apr. 15th, 1679† [— Mason intruded]		,, ,,
1679	John Wickes, S.T.B.		,, ,,
1684	Wm. Hughes, M.A.†		,, ,,
1699	Ric. Allyn, S.T.B.†		,, ,,
1733	James Muscut, M.A.†		,, ,,
1758	Edward Towersey, B.D.†		,, ,,
1776	John Keble, M.A.	resigned	,, ,,
1782	Humphrey Smythies, M.A.†		,, ,,
1806	John Emeris, B.D.†		,, ,,
1831	Francis Robinson, M.A.	resigned	,, ,,
1881	Henry Gordon Cranmer, B.A.†		,, ,,
1899	Alfred Arthur Hancock, M.A.		,, ,,

Picture II
Thomas Annie & Clarabel going on their way.
Annie & Clarabel facing us – very agitated.
Suggest a variation of
The Tank Engine Thomas P7 or P13
But please remember Thomas is propelling the train brake first – he is not pulling it – be careful of smoke showing direction of travel.

Picture III The Mine is near DRYAW (See sketch map of the Branch Line which I made and sent you for Tank Engine Thomas again

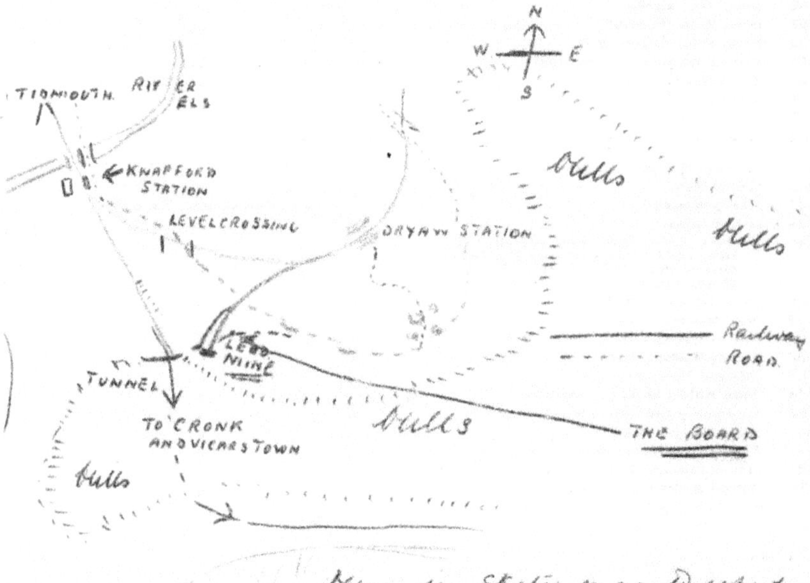

Here is sketch map to refresh your memory.
Thomas goes up to Farquhar (at the end of the Branch Line – leaves Annie & Clarabel

will be travelling to the mine from Farquhar

<u>Funnel first</u>

I suggest picture on these lines

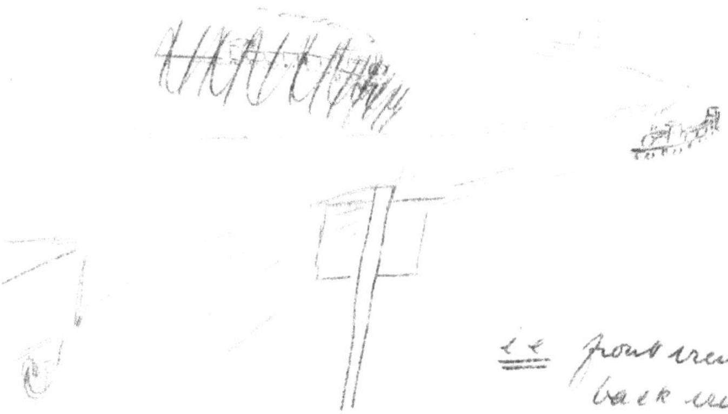

i.e. front view of Thomas
back view of notice.

Picture IV <u>Back view</u> of Thomas, and <u>front view</u> of notice

Thomas has run round his trucks and is <u>pushing</u> them into their siding.
- Fireman having turned points waves Thomas on
- Thomas jerks driver off – driver sitting on ground feeling self for bruises
- Thomas follows trucks past the board into the siding leaving driver behind.

<u>Picture V</u> Front view of Thomas well past the board looking pleased. Fireman ~~[illegible]~~ running to jump up on foot plate – Driver in back ground frantically waving them back.

You can see how my father's illustrations had improved over time.

Picture VI Front view - Thomas sunk in hole.
His front is tilted downwards & his
bunker up. This sort of idea. - plenty
of people about - sheds
mine buildings. it is a lead

Picture VII Gordon pulling Thomas out.
Front view Gordon rear view Thomas
Cables must be long enough to allow
Gordon to be well on the safe side of
the board.
Fat Controller giving directions
Gordon puffs with effort.
Thomas just coming out of the hole.
& on level ground again.

Picture VIII Thomas & Gordon going to Ranmouth
Gordon & Thomas coupled together
buffer to buffer - both in reverse.
[illegible]

As the stories developed so too did the many locations around the Island of Sodor which was no different to any of the other railway networks facing modernisation up and down the country, well except the fact that on the Island lived talking engines and coaches! Here you can see some of the changes to the stations and features of Sodor that Father was constantly evolving as the stories developed.

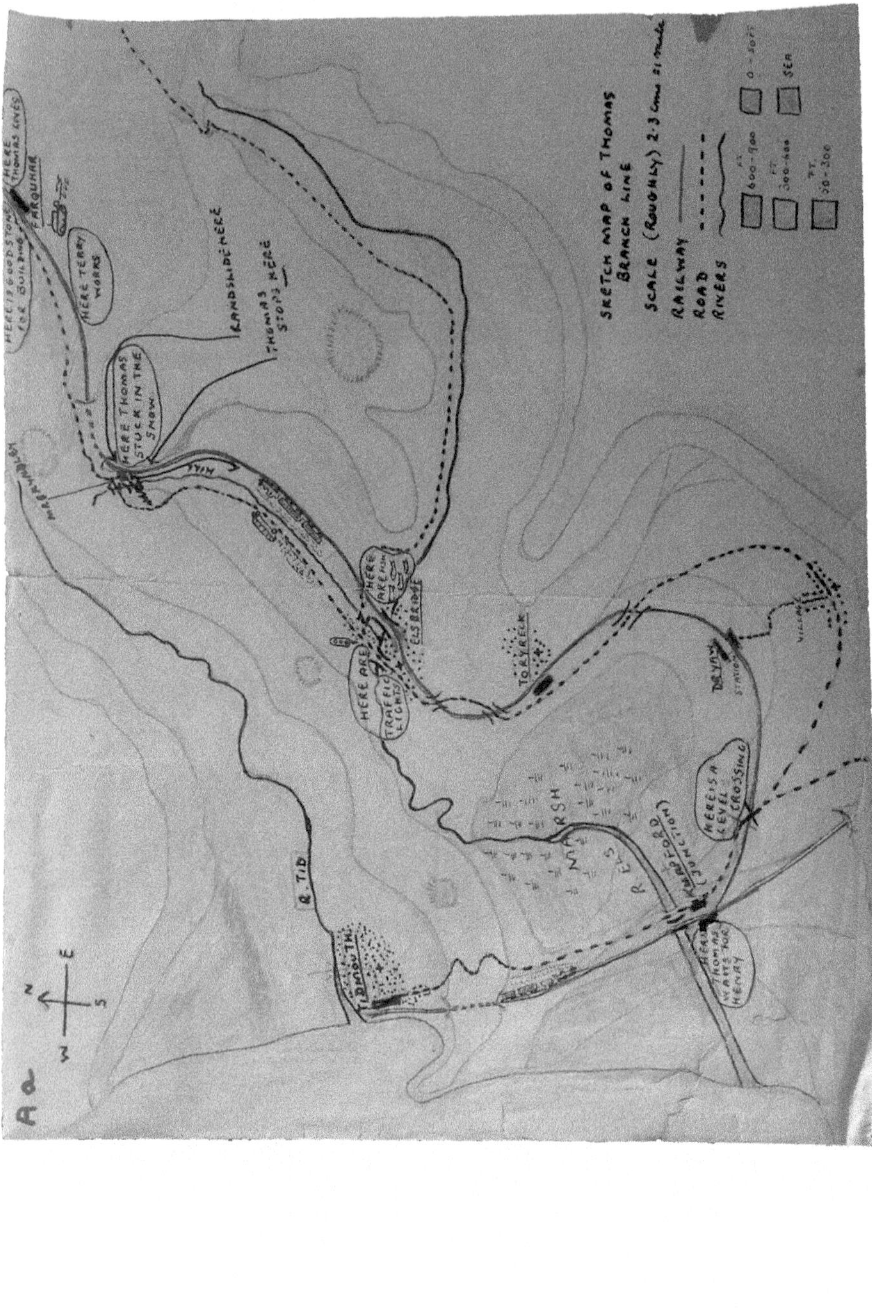

A sketch map drawn by my father to prove to his children that the race between Thomas and Bertie from *Tank Engine Thomas Again* was indeed quite fair as both had the same amount of hazards to negotiate!

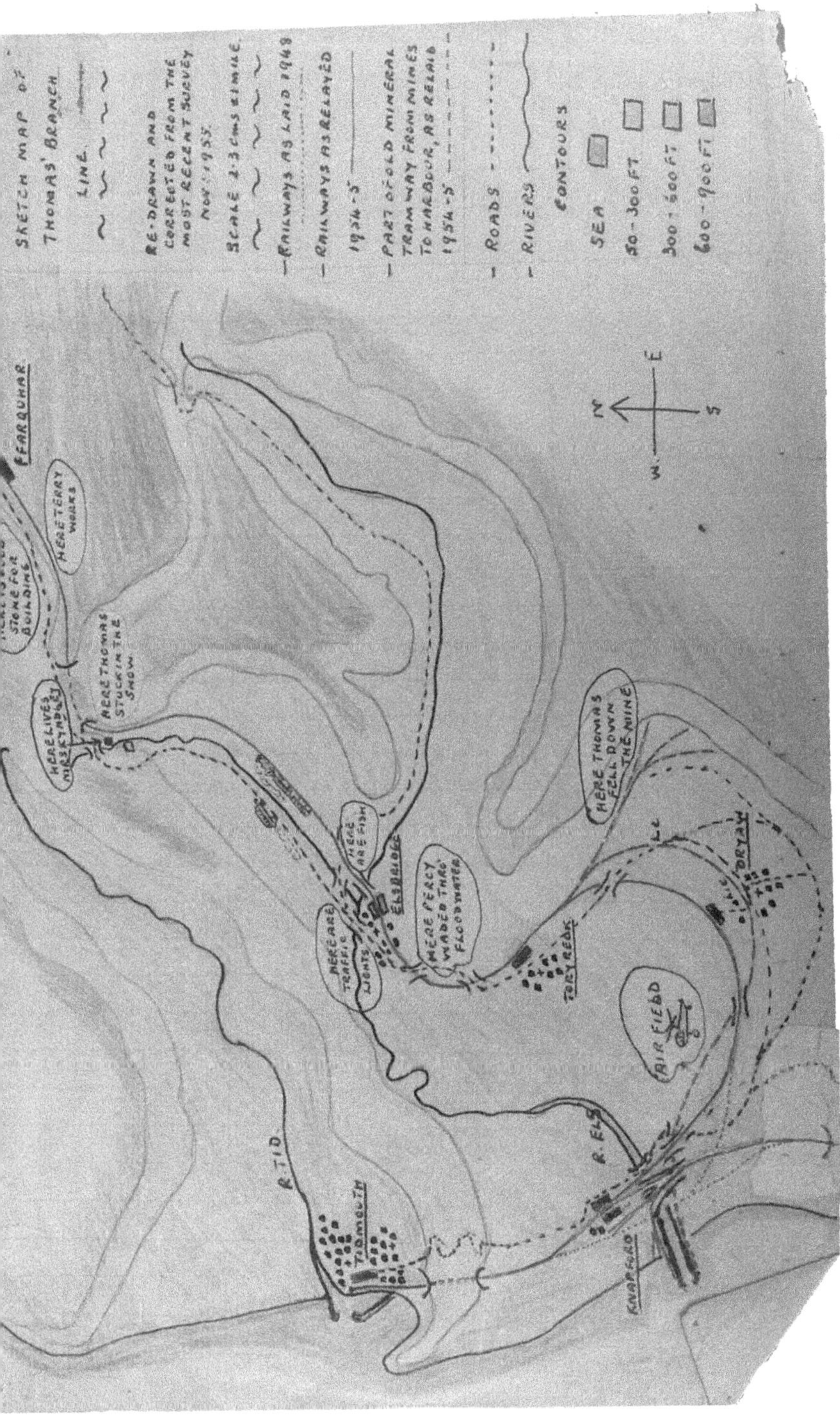

As the stories expanded, the locations did too. Here we have an updated version of the map on the previous page that was drawn by one of Father's friends for an article in the 'Railway Modeller.' The pencil lines denote developments renderred necessary by subsequent stories.

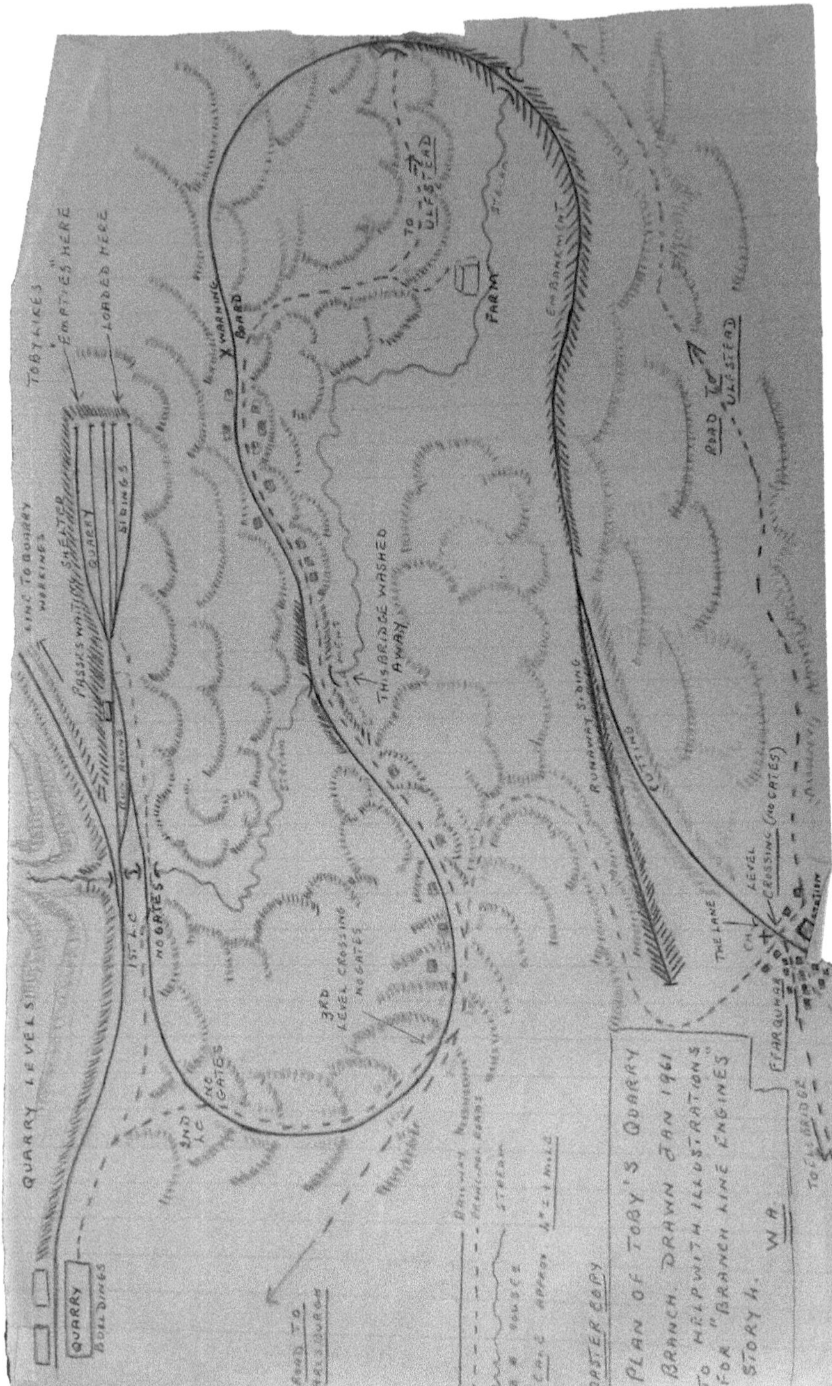

Father's drawing of the Roadside Tramway to the Anopha Quarry. Drawn originally for Dalby's benefit when illustrating Stories in *Toby the Tram Engine* then revised in 1961 for Branch Line Engines before finally helping Peter Edwards when illustrating *Tramway Engines*.

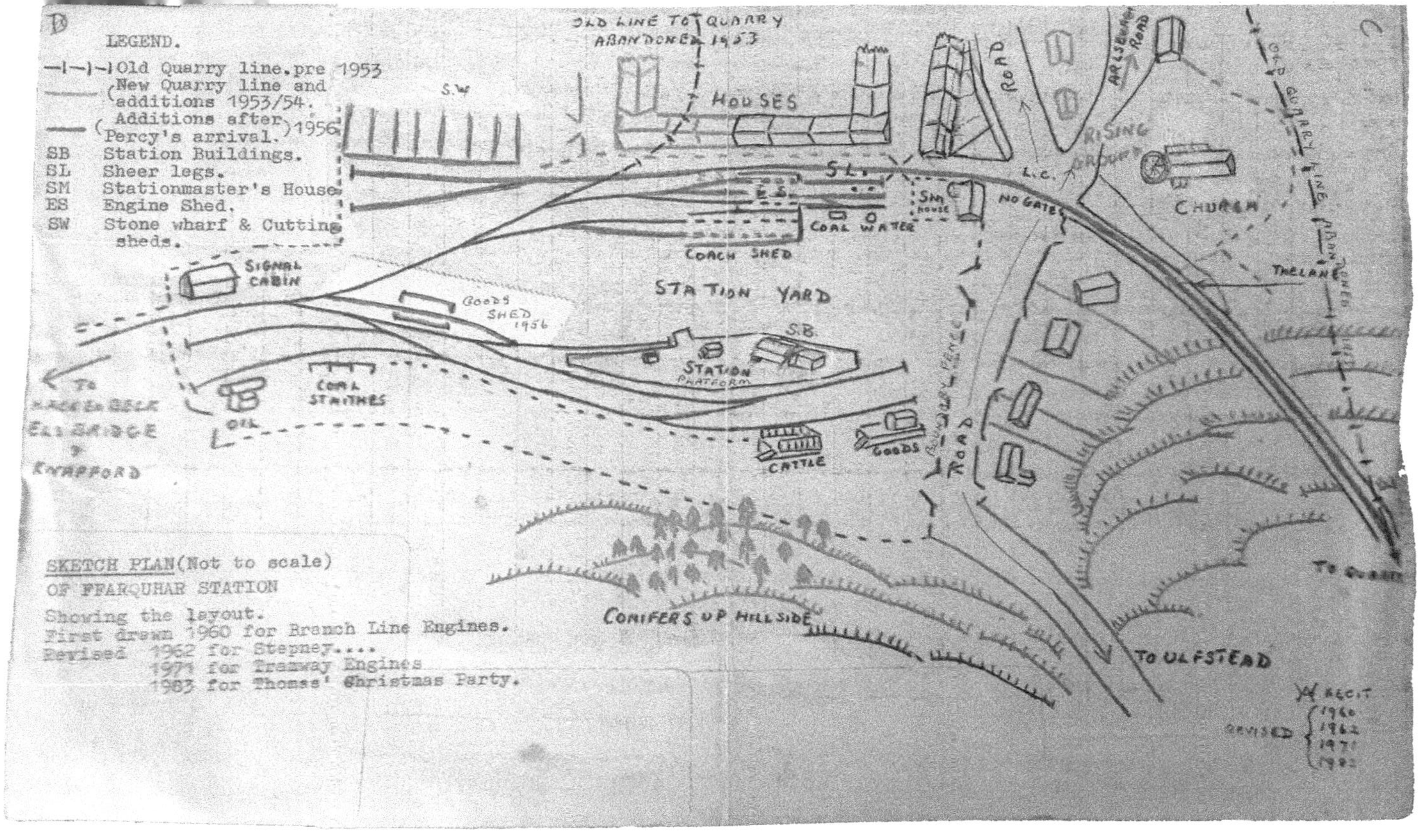

This map shows the layout of the Ffarquhar Station and town. Drawn originally in 1960 to help John Kenney with his illustrations of *Branch Line Engines*. This was based on Father's Ffarquhar station of his Mark 1 model, but due to size limitations the model could not be used to show things such as the Stone Yard, Carriage and Engine Sheds and Stationmaster's house etc. You can see it has been revised over time to accomodate the later stories including the 1983 *Thomas' Christmas Party*.

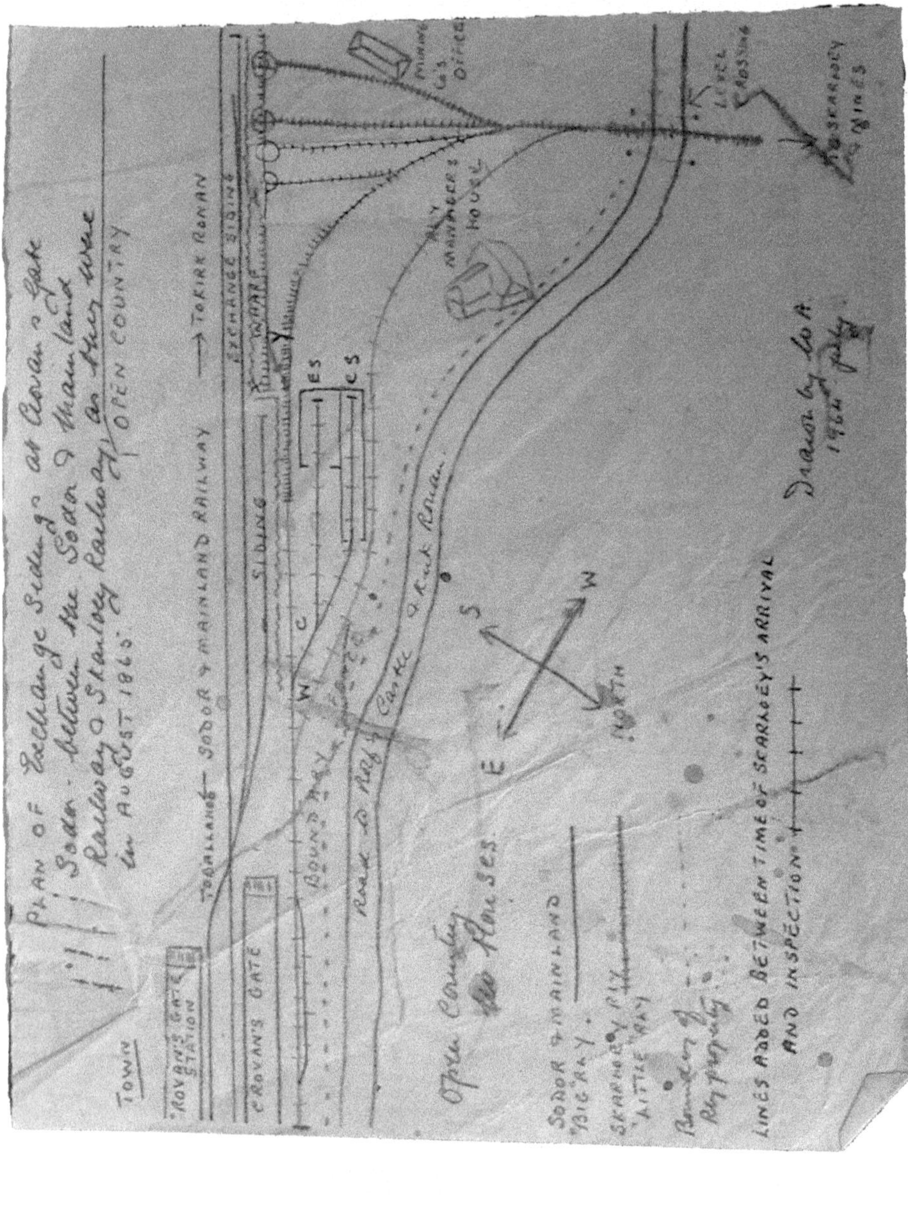

As you can read for yourself, this is a plan of the Exchange sidings at Crovan's Gate, drawn by Father in July 1964.

Let's go all scenic with this one.
Duck and his two coaches Alice and Mirabelle
travelling along a sea-side stretch of line.
If you have a picture of a scenic bit along
the Cambrian coast that would do very well as
basis. The stretch I have in mind would be
somewhere between Aberdovey and Barmouth (NOT
Barmouth bridge - that is too unique) or
between Harlech and Penrhyndeudraeth, or even
between Criccieth and Pwllheli.
DUCK will be as usual
ALICE
MIRABELLE) will be G. Western autocoaches like
Isabel in Enterprising engines, but
painted in G. Western colours
Yellowish cream upper panels, and
dark chocolate lower panels.
N.B. There was an oversight here in last picture
of Enterprising engines where lower panels
were shown as a shade of red. I am expecting
a number of letters pointing out the mistake
particularly as the text says full Great
Western colours. I shall have a lot of
'explaining' to do after Nov 11th!

Picture notes from *Donald's Duck* that originally my Father wanted to call *Little Western Engines* interesting to note (above) that he already pre-empted fans to write in about the mistake.

PICTURE NOTES

Two suggestions.

(a) Donald out somewhere on the main line with
a goods train - actual location unimportant -
except that it should appear to be a biggish
traffic centre
Henry, Gordon, or James or
any two winking at each other and laughing
at the comical apparition in Donald's
tender and the sounds proceeding therefrom.

(b) Fireman has caught duckling after first
appearance from the tank. He, holding it,
has taken it round to Donald's front to
show it to him.
Donald is laughing - he knows who is
responsible - Driver and Fireman are
still a bit surprised, as well they
might be.

(c) A third suggestion. Cab scene during their
dinner break.
Driver and Fireman sitting one each side
of cab feeding the duckling with bits
from their sandwiches. Duckling stands
expectant between them, not sure from
which side the next bit is going to
come.

N.B. (c) is a nice picture, but will involve quite a bit of cab
interior detail, and also a picture quite similar
is suggested for page 7, as one of three alternatives.

My Personal preference would be for (b)

Picture notes for *Toad Stands By*. You can see here the level of detail that Father insisted upon from the illustrator.

OLIVER THE WESTERN ENGINE by Rev.W.Awdry.

Story III Toad stands by.

Picture 1. Footbridge. See my remarks for story II picture 5. There I suggested abolishing it, but with this picture in mind I am inclined <u>to keep it</u> but make it longer. and <u>lower</u>, abolish arch effect & make it straight across. then signals both for arrival & departure can be put in. Its present width suggests that shunting operations such as are shown in this picture take up main line to passenger platforms as well. This would not do for Sir Topham Hatt!

Making bridge longer will suggest that there is another road into the passenger platform. Bridge need not be higher than it is immediately behind Duck.

Nice arrangement otherwise.

Picture 2. Toad looks much too squat. Buffer beams and fromes too low. vehicle is drawn either too wide or else not long enough. Check proportions in the photograph I sent you.

Picture 3. Nice arrangement but.
- Engine shed. see notes on same for Story I
- Oliver. Expression rather 'forbidding'

Picture 4. Nice arrangement generally, but
- Scruffy looks as though he is being propelled straight at Duck! Could we have his far end round a little more to right to show that he really is going along the same line as the other trucks.
- Oliver. Same thing applies here.
- Buffer beams. by the size of the shunter. These would appear to be a little low. Reduce size of shunter till buffers are <u>chest height</u>, not waist height.
- Engine shed. Corner showing. make sure it matches up.

Picture 5 Good in General.
- Scruffy. The effect suggested in the picture is an explosion! When all that has really happened is that the front part of the wagon has given way under tension.

Hope this very rough sketch gives the idea.
- Duck Has just arrived back so (N.B. also in picture 4) he will have <u>tail lamp</u>

Picture 6. Nice general arrangement but,
- Wagon remains. These will have been picked up and dumped somewhere as shown. What however is the man examining. Are they wagon slebars. If so he must be a 'Sampson' to pick up and hold two halves of same in each hand. Play safe instead and have him looking closely at wreckage and not handl[illegible] it. He could be in centre of picture & F.C. on right [illegible] back towards us [illegible] & facing Oliver.

The original description of Duck

Here are two Photos which will show what the Duck looks like.
He is a G.W.R.Pannier Tank of the '5700' class.
Colour details
Tanks, Boiler mountings, Cabfront and sides , bunker, and front of Tanks Great Western green, Dome and safety valve are also this colour.
WHeels, Smoke-box door, Funnel, side-frames, Splashers and all side detail below the Tanks, also Cab roof, are Black
Coupling rods, polished steel.
Buffer heads, and shanks , polished steel

Buffer beams and sockets red.

Until further notice. That is until the Fat Controller orders otherwise Duck continues to carry the Letters G.W.R. as shown on the sides of his tanks. These letters are Gold. shaded with red.

He also till further notice carries his Great Western number plate (Black background, brass raised 'surround' and numerals. The numerals will normally be too small to be distinguished, but if they can be distinguished at any time they should be 5741.

NOTE That in the two photos supplied the shape, and size of the boiler mountings Viz Funnel, Dome, safety valve differ Persomally, from the point of view of looks, I prefer those on the lower picture particularly the funnel.

For the purpose of our illustration, I would suggest that the Fat controller be shown talking to the Duck on his arrival. Location can be anywhere in the Yard. Perhaps Percy could be sh shown in the back-ground and F.C. might be waving to Percy, calling him to come and show Duck round.

A letter from my father to the editor of E Ward Publishers.
Here you can see the discussion for the title of book 22 *Small Railway Engines*

Sodor
Rodborough Avenue
Stroud

1/Nov/66

Dear Mr Marriott,

Thankyou for your two letters which were awaiting our return yesterday. Incidentally We spent two days at St Austell where we had a great welcome at the China Clay works and the Port of Par. They seem quite delighted that two engines similar to theirs are appearing in one of the books. When are they due out by the way? Would you please send me a dozen copies in addition to the ½doz Author's complimentaries.

Now about the 1967 book. Title. You suggest three:-

(a) Small Railway Engines
(b) Minature Engines
(c) Lakeside Engines. I note that you prefer (c). I agree that it is simple and direct. But all the same we can't use it because it is inaccurate. The Arlsdale Railway is no more near any lakes than the Ravenglass and Eskdale. besides, it is not in Cumberland, it is in Sodor. Of the three you suggest I prefer (a). (b) Minature engines is good and succinct but it has a somewhat pedantic sound, and I should not think that your sales representatives would like it very much. However I don't really mind which it is (a) or (b) but (c) is right out. Besides being innaccurate it gives the ~~impression~~ suggestion of being one of those rather footling little railways in an amusement park.

I enclose, for yourself and Peter Edwards a brief outline of the background of the whole thing which has had to be worked out carefully before any of the stories could be written. I also enclose a copy of the map on which I have indicated the various developments which have occurred. I have not put them in accurately. That is impossible because the map itself is innaccurate, but I have sufficiently indicated their position.

With best wishes

Yours sincerely

W. Awdry

Over the next three pages you can see Father's notes to Peter Edwards with regards illustrations for Mike's Whistle. Again, you can see my father's meticulous attention to detail.

SMALL RAILWAY ENGINES Story III Mike's Whistle Notes on Roughs

Picture I. Nice arrangement gets just the effect needed

Points of detail.

Cradle Tipping arrangement. Remove please

Duck. Safety valve and dome. Not quite the right shape. This is more obvious in a 'close-up' such as this than in other pictures

Whistles . All Great Western engines had two whistles. One small with high pitched tone for ordinary use. One large and deep toned to give the alarm in emergencies (brakes etc). They were arranged side by side between safety valve and cab.

The Small one had a cap 4½" high and 2¼" diameter (outside measurements)

The large one's cap was 5" high and 3¼" diameter (outside measurements)

I have been unable to find a close-up detailed photo so send you this book of drawings. The general arrangement with shape of dome, safety valve cover etc is on page 62

The whistles are drawn to a larger scale right hand bottom corner of page ~~62~~ 81.

Mike. Bring smokebox front forward a bit. Not enough overhang from saddle.

N.B. This story will set young readers searching for the whistles on the other engines as well. Make sure that both Rex and Bert have theirs in all other pictures, and arranged properly too.

Rex's is vertical, but Bert's is arranged horizontally, examination of photos of Rivers Esk and Irt will show the arrangement. Mike's is vertical, as drawing shows.

Please check roughs of stories I & II for whistles.

Picture II. Good general arrangement. A few small points though.

Mike. Bring smokebox and chimney forward a little. There is not enough overhang from smokebox saddle in front. Hence gives impression of too much Front End.

Bert. Steam pipes too large (from smokebox to cylinders) N.B. Inside frames, siderods, massive cranks.

Cabs of all three don't look quite right.

Picture III Good effect of a "rough start" by Mike.

N.B. siderods & valve gear

Firebox. Sides come out at an angle not vertical as shown here.

No number please on cab side.

Picture IV. A good general effect. But with Mike right across foreground, I had to stop and think what this picture was about. It is not immediately clear, because, naturally enough, you did not sketch in the details of the Turntable.

One point. The railway staff ~~always~~ always push locomotives round from the tender end. They have probably learnt the hard way that the front end of an engine is hot!

So, could we have the Guard removed from the front and pushing, or at least taking a 'breather' from pushing at the tender end. He could be taking his 'breather' while Driver does his examination.

NOTES ON ROUGHS

STORY III CONTINUED MIKE'S WHISTLE

Picture 5. Nice arrangement. The cow is delightful.

Shape of whistle cap. Close examination of loco photographs, and of the River Mite drawing shows that cap is not the shape shown 'in orbit' in the rough.

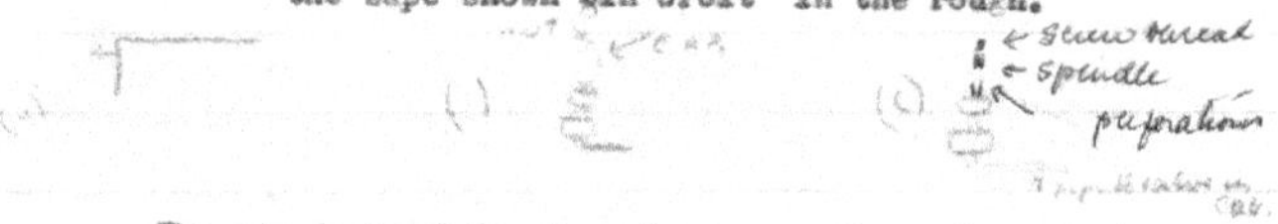

The cap is held in place by means of a nut screwed on to the threaded central spindle. The steam is conveyed to the whistle by a pipe from the cab which when it reaches a point inside the cap is perforated. The cap fastening spindle is(I imagine) welded inside the steam pipe at a point above the perforations, thus corking it up and providing at the same time a fastening for the cap.

Unfortunately I omitted to examine a whistle dismantled, but that is my guess as to how it is arranged.

Path of whistle cap . Would be such as shown first. I do not imagine it would loop the loop

Further. I think steam at 120 lbs per square inch as coming direct from boiler would(for some distance at least) go straight up.

Remains of whistle on engine after the cap went into orbit would be as shown in sketch (c) above.

Mike's ~~sxxxx~~ buffers drawing seems to show a slightly oval shape. Your rough shows them round. Please check with other drawings, and though I don't mind which they are, oval or round, please be consistent through out book

If you aren't I shall be bombarded endlessly by sharp eyed correspondents!

This happened with Gordon and Henry!

No number please on cab side.

Picture 6. WHISTLE BOARDS are placed in advance (¼ mile or so) of Level Crossings. and NEVER at stations. I am sorry but this one won't do.

There is an opportunity here for an attractive country scenic picture.

Three suggestions offered. Photos I & II enclosed or III the cover picture of the Handbook.

If you use I. The direction of the train would have to be reversed, and view point shifted more to the right, so as to get a view of Mike and his expression. Further coaches would need to be added on left, in place of River Irt. *attractive wooded background* *Hollinghow before cutting*

II. Use train as it is, with Mike instead of River IRT, back of Whistle board inserted on right, and cut out some 2½ inches of foreground. Viz lines on margin each side. *Impressive mountain scenery.* *approaching Ealbar's cutting from level.*

III. Use picture as it is, substituting Mike for Irt, and putting in back of whistle board on right of track (left, facing direction of travel) *Good value scenically*

STORY III MIKE'S WHISTLE.

Picture 1. Duck's expression very nice. You have managed the whistles well
Please check shape of CHIMNEY. It tapers too much here.
Mike. Indicate nameplate please.
THAS are not served either, in the Small Controller's Office!

2. A VERY PLEASANT PICTURE INDEED This is an alternative for the Jacket.
Two points. (a) Position of nameplates for each of the three engines, should be above handrail.
Mike. Edges of frames red please, not blue, except the two small bits in line with smokebox front. Make these black please.

3. Good & dramatic picture.
Two points though (a) Mike's sideframes red not blue.
(b) Mike's firebox shape does not fit with other pictures, or the drawing I sent at the beginning The sides come out AT AN ANGLE AS I POINTED OUT IN THE NOTES ON THE ROUGH. YOU HAVE MADE THEM VERTICAL LIKE BERT'S. Please alter it to fit in with rest of pictures in the book in the manner of this rough sketch.

(c) Hand rail, Blower pipe, nameplate positions do not correspond with the official drawing. please check this point in all pictures.

4. Very nice, much improved.
But, please compare position of 'run-round' track in this picture with that of same in story II picture 5. Story II picture 5 looks better so please alter this picture.
One other point. The track as drawn here, looks much too narrow. Compare it with all the other pictures so far drawn.
Nameplate very nice but please brass letters on black or dark blue background.
Edges of frames, red not blue please.
Makes plate on Cab Side

That I'm afraid brings us to the end of our peek behind the curtain. "What!" I hear you cry, "but what about this character, or that station, or that engine?" Like I said at the beginning of this chapter, not every question will, should or can be answered. Sometimes it's nice to have a little 'mystery' behind a story, especially one that is now 80 years old and counting.

I do hope you have enjoyed seeing some of my father's correspondence with key people along the way, allowing you a unique insight into Father's thoughts over the years.

I'd also like to take this opportunity to thank all of the many volunteers up and down our country who spend their time helping to keep the many preserved Railways open, some of which only survive thanks to either generous donations from the public or through the hard work and commitment of people willing to give up their free time. We've been blessed to have visited many of them on our travels and tours, and all made us feel very welcome. So thank you for all your hard work and effort.

That dear friends, readers and fans of The Railway Series, is now where I, like my father before me, bid you farewell. Thank you for supporting Sodor Reading Between the Lines and my other works and for all the support, well wishes, and loyalty over the years.

God Bless you all.

Love, peace and prosperity,

Christopher.

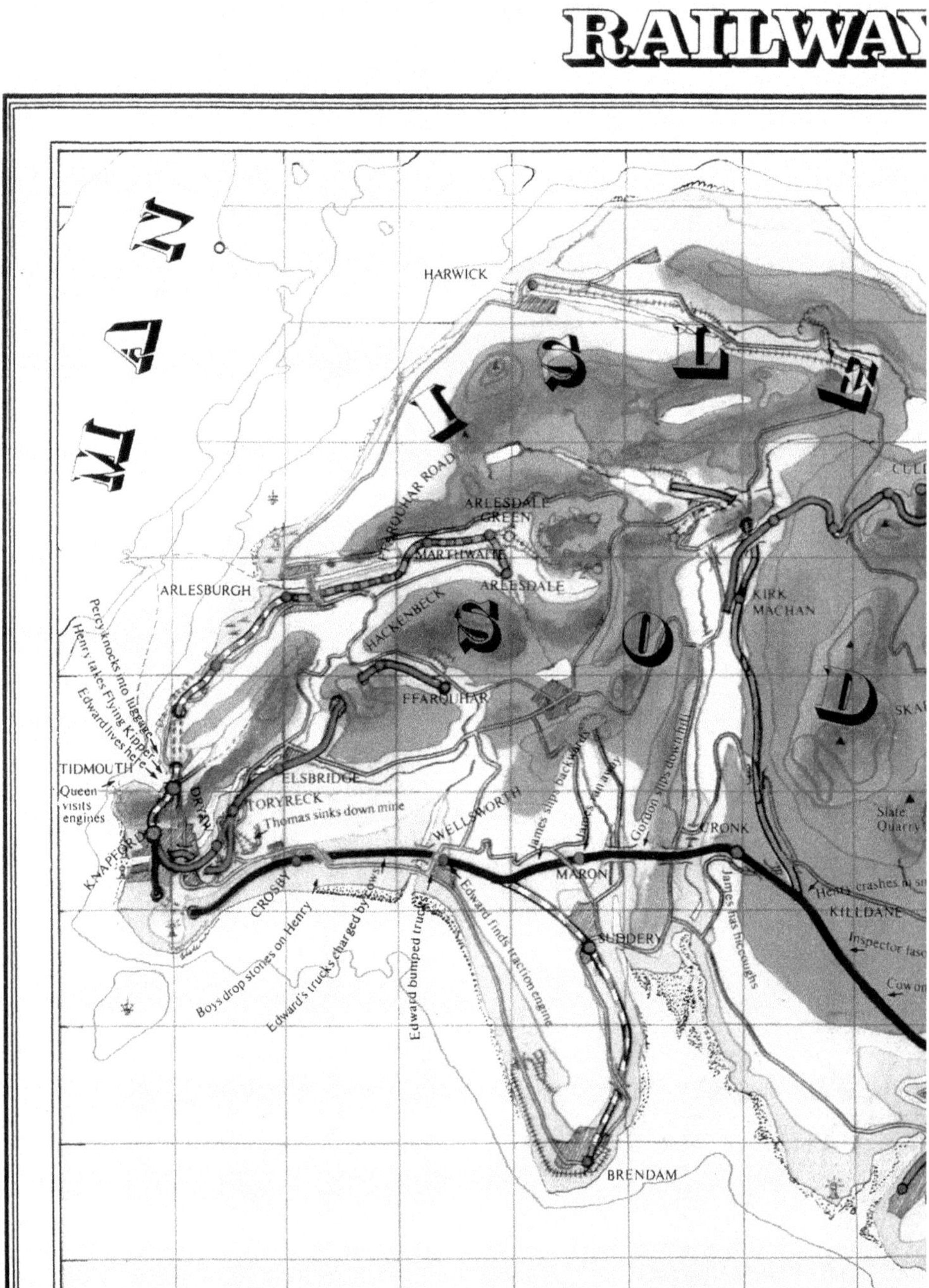
RAILWAY
ISLE OF SODOR
HARWICK
FFARQUHAR ROAD
ARLESDALE GREEN
MARTHWAITE
ARLESDALE
ARLESBURGH
HACKENBECK
FFARQUHAR
KIRK MACHAN
TIDMOUTH
Queen visits engines
Percy knocks into luggage
Henry takes Flying Kipper
Edward lives here
KNAPFORD
DRYAW
ELSBRIDGE
TORYRECK
Thomas sinks down mine
WELLSWORTH
James slips backwards
Gordon slips down hill
CRONK
MARON
CROSBY
Boys drop stones on Henry
Edward finds traction engine
Edward bumped trucks
SUDDERY
James has hiccoughs
KILLDANE
Slate Quarry
BRENDAM

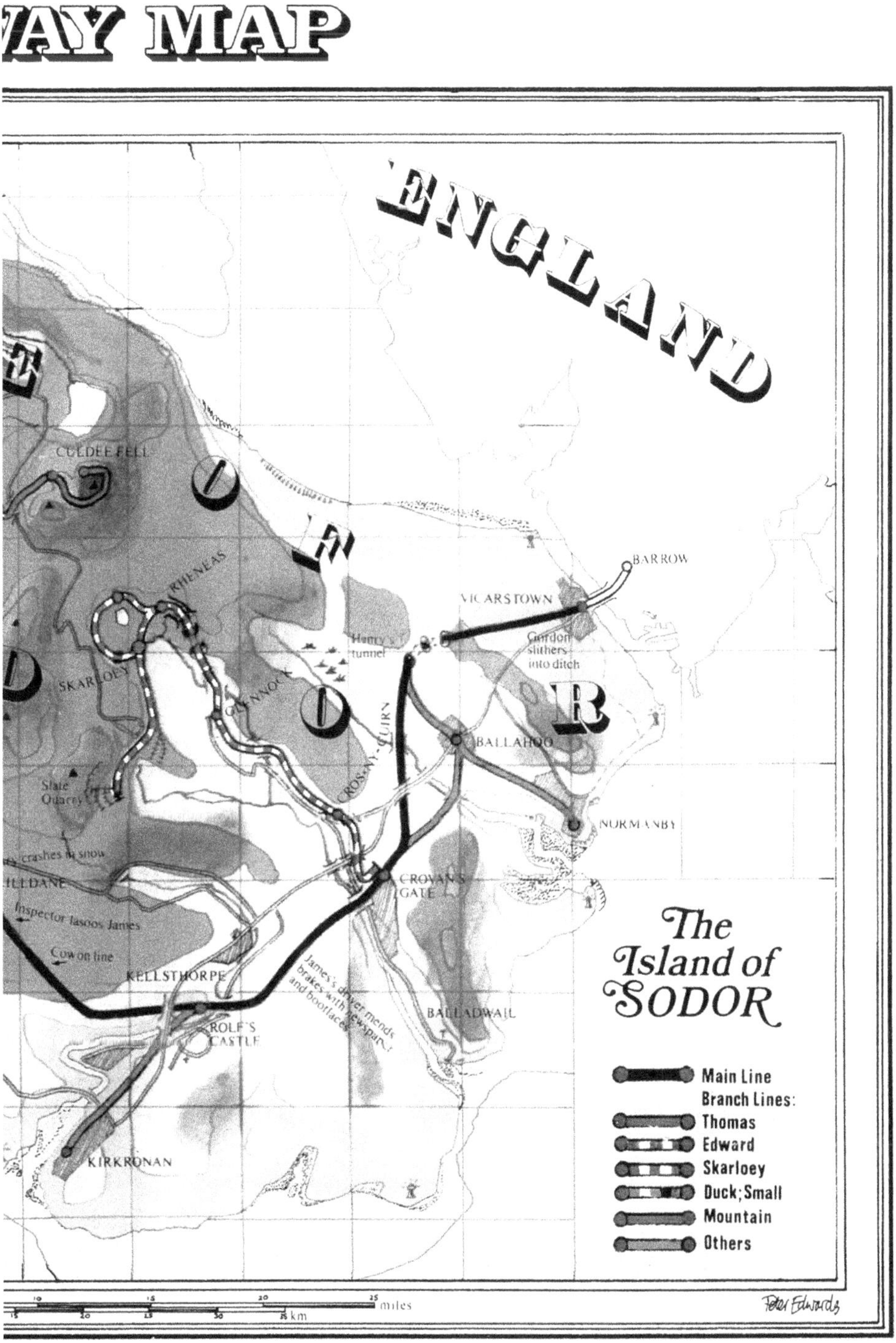
AY MAP
ENGLAND
CULDEE FELL
RHENEAS
SKARLOEY
GLENNOCK
Slate Quarry
Henry's tunnel
VICARSTOWN
BARROW
Gordon slithers into ditch
BALLAHOO
NORMANBY
CROVAN'S GATE
crashes in snow
Cow on line
KELLSTHORPE
ROLF'S CASTLE
James's driver mends brakes with newspapers and bootlaces
BALLADWAIL
KIRKRONAN
The Island of SODOR
Main Line
Branch Lines:
Thomas
Edward
Skarloey
Duck; Small
Mountain
Others
miles
km
Peter Edwards

www.ingramcontent.com/pod-product-compliance
Ingram Content Group UK Ltd.
Pitfield, Milton Keynes, MK11 3LW, UK
UKHW031823260826
14628UKWH00001B/188

9 781919 309309